Shapiro's Plan

"You're a good lawyer, Nick. I know what you can do in the courtroom. You can win it on your own."

"Win, the future's clear. Lose...."

"You've got the guts, Nick."

"Or I could sell hot dogs downtown from a pushcart."

"Decide, Nick."

"I can win this case on my own."

"Is that the plan, Nick?"

He didn't answer.

Shapiro's Plan

by
Michael Lechtman

Commonwealth
Publications

A Commonwealth Publications Paperback
SHAPIRO'S PLAN

This edition published 1996
by Commonwealth Publications
9764 - 45th Avenue,
Edmonton, AB, CANADA T6E 5C5
All rights reserved
Copyright © 1995 by Michael Lechtman

ISBN: 1-55197-282-4

This work is a novel and any similarity to actual persons or events is purely coincidental.

Designed by: Danielle Monlezun

Printed in Canada

For my mother, Beatrice.
Her sons love her very much.

PART I

CHAPTER 1

Neal Shapiro banked left on the stretch of inter-state that surrounded the tall buildings of down-town. The Harris County Courthouse used to be the most prominent tower in the area, but now it could barely be seen, hidden as it was amongst the new chrome and glass skyscrapers that dwarfed it like a toadstool on the forest floor. The Texaco station next to the courthouse was gone, too. Shapiro remembered when lawyers could leave their cars there in exchange for a fill-up of gas. Now he had to park near the river flats, six blocks away. He had grown weary of the walk.

"Five bucks," the attendant said through the open car window, "in advance."

Shapiro studied the man who was wearing jeans and a white tee-shirt. He couldn't tell if the man was young or old: the way the sun had dried his skin.

"In advance? You've got my car for security," Shapiro said.

"Ain't my decision, mister, owner sets the rules. Parking or not?"

Shapiro dug into his pocket, clearing away some coins and a credit card holder before getting to the paper money.

"I'll need a receipt."

The attendant pulled a pencil from behind his ear, scribbled the date on a preprinted pad and tore off a sheet.

"Gets you two hours. Another five bucks after that."

"If I stay any longer, I'll just let you keep the car."

The attendant didn't seem to hear. He sat down in a folding chair that was propped up against a wooden hut and dialed a number on his cellular phone.

Shapiro drove in and parked. He opened his trunk and took out his briefcase and his suitcoat, which he slung over his shoulder by a hooked finger. He headed north on Galtier Street, his tired feet dragging on the pavement in the heat.

There was a new smell on the streets of downtown from food pushcarts: Mexican, Caribbean barbecue, Chinese, pizza, falafel. There were even hot dog carts for those who still wanted to eat American.

A young woman with long legs, high heels and a bikini bathing suit that looked more like dental floss was selling hot dogs at the corner of Galtier and Strand.

Shapiro walked up to her.

"Make any money at this?" Shapiro asked.

She finished turning some franks on the grill, then reached into a drawer and came out with a business card.

"A ton. I franchise too...initial investment's five thousand. Of course, I make a lot more than most of my franchisees."

"I'll bet," Shapiro said.

He handed her his business card.

She read it, her lips moving.

"Why would a lawyer be interested in buying a pushcart?" she asked.

"It's got to be better than practicing law." Shapiro slipped into his jacket, then turned and crossed the street against the light. A taxi he didn't notice had to brake hard to avoid hitting him.

The woman waved Shapiro's card in the air.

"Mr. Shapiro!" She tried to call out above the noise of the traffic. "There's a special rate if you buy more than one pushcart."

Her breasts bounced as she spoke. Soon she was surrounded by hungry men in business suits.

Shapiro walked north three more blocks and took a left on Remington, where the Harris County Courthouse jumped out like a naughty boy who'd been hiding from his father. Its chiseled lines and 1930's architecture copied the great buildings of Rockefeller Center in New York, making it the only building in view that still spoke of old-fashioned business.

There was a steep bank of steps leading up to the lobby. No longer did Shapiro leap up the staircase two stairs at a time. He did that his first time at the courthouse twenty-five years ago. How long had it been since he'd gone up those steps like that? He passed by a group of bailiffs in white shirts and badges who were taking a cigarette break outside. Most didn't smoke anymore. None of them looked familiar, except for Eddie Tyler, the right-hand man of Chief Judge Henry Finer.

The experienced bailiff stepped out of the crowd.

"Hello, Nick," he said.

"Eddie, what's new?"

"Haven't seen you around; you're looking kind of tired."

"I work out sometimes...got nothing better to do."

"You go to the gym to see those tight little tushes on the young girls."

Eddie was probably right.

"Take it easy, Eddie."

"Take it any way I can get it."

Shapiro headed for the revolving doors.

His first name was Neal. He had hated it when he was a kid and had always liked Nick better. Now only his wife called him Neal.

The two women working the metal detector spoke to each other in a language Shapiro didn't understand. They didn't seem to be looking at the TV monitor at all, too engrossed in their conversation. He could have had an AK-47 in his briefcase for all they seemed to care.

Shapiro didn't remove the wad of keys from his pocket before passing through the machine.

There was no electronic bleep.

The four elevators in the courthouse were never working all at once. Today there was only one functioning. When the car came, a horde of lawyers, most of them women, pushed their way in. Shapiro and three other male lawyers didn't make it onto the elevator.

"The fairer sex," one of the lawyers said.

"It's what's happened to the profession," said the one with all-white hair and a mustache to match. "There was more respect for lawyers before *they* took over."

Shapiro cringed. If only his wife, Marilee, had heard. She would have hit the old boy over the head with his umbrella. Hadn't he ever heard the term "politically correct?"

The elevator came down again, and the men got on. After making a stop on every level, Shapiro exited on the fourteenth floor. He went to Judge Cindy Gievers' chambers. The note on the locked door read: "calendar call in courtroom 14-1." It was the small courtroom at the end of the hall.

Shapiro entered and took a seat in the second row of the empty jury box. He checked the wall clock: 12:45. In all his years of practice he'd never been late for a court appearance. Fifteen minutes early was his standard.

Only one other lawyer was in the room, a man sitting at the counsel table reading through a thick file. Shapiro didn't know who he was. There was a time when that couldn't have been possible. All the lawyers used to know each other by their first names.

A calendar call is something conducted by the judges on the Thursday before a trial week begins. The lawyers on both sides of a case are required to be present to advise the judge if they're ready for trial, how long the trial will take and whether any possible problems could be settled. Then numbers would be assigned for the order in which the cases would be tried. It was the lawyer's duty to stay in touch with the case ahead of them in order to see when their case would be called. Because no one ever knew exactly how many days it would take to try a given case, and since some cases settled during trial, it was impossible to maintain a semblance of an office schedule if you were a trial lawyer.

It was one of the reasons why most lawyers didn't do trial work.

The ones that did usually died young.

Brothers and sisters of the bar began filling the courtroom. By one o'clock nearly every seat had been taken. All that was missing was the judge and her staff. As Cindy Gievers was a new judge, Shapiro had never tried a case before her.

The room grew noisy with conversation, like a

high school class when the teacher was out of the room. Was that what this group was, kids?

Shapiro examined the backs of his hands. He looked at the few small liver spots that had started and noticed the graying hair on his forearms. He was the oldest lawyer in the courtroom. He studied the faces of the other lawyers; not one was familiar. The men looked like they were going to a school dance, dressed in new suits, red cheeked, with skin so smooth it didn't seem like they had to shave. The women looked even younger, despite their high heels.

"I've got my first jury trial coming up next week," the woman in the row in front of Shapiro said to her friend.

"It's a trip; you'll love it," the friend said. "What're you doing this weekend?"

"I don't know, maybe go the jazz concert out at Fleigle's Saturday afternoon."

"Have a date?"

"Who would I want to go out with?"

"Maybe I'll go with you."

"What'll you wear?"

"Something sexy, I may get lucky."

Shapiro waited for them to laugh. No one did. He thought it was a joke.

"How do you do it, anyhow, a jury trial?"

"Same as nonjury, except you've got to pick the jury, be on your feet more. There's supposed to be an art to it, but I can't see it. In England they just take the first six people in the box, a lot less work that way."

The other woman shrugged her shoulders.

"Do you like my hair this way?"

Her friend started leafing through the frosted curls with her fingers.

"A little shorter maybe, but not too much. The

front's cute, I like that."

Shapiro slouched down in his seat, and lifted his briefcase to his knees so he could hide his face behind the open lid. Who were these people? He had carried Mel Forman's briefcase around for five years learning what they don't teach students in law school. Jury selection was everything. Forman had shown him the craft. What was happening here?

The woman with the frosted hair took a bottle of pink nail polish from her purse. When she began to apply it, the smell permeated the room.

"Where's the judge?" she asked her friend.

"Cindy had a luncheon at the Bay Club. She told me last night she'd be a little late."

"You know her?"

"Went to school together. She asked me if she should excuse herself from any cases I have before her, and I told her, hell no, let my opponent figure it out."

"God, it must be wonderful having a judge like that."

"Get better tables at restaurants, too."

A door opened on the side of the room. A bailiff entered. He tried to make his voice sound deep. "All rise. Circuit court in and for Harris County is now in session. The Honorable Cindy Gievers presiding."

The judge, who had frosted hair just like her friend, followed behind the bailiff. Her black judicial robes were too big for her, allowing the garment to remain steady while her little body bounced beneath it.

The judge sat.

"Be seated," she said to the room. "This is the trial calendar for next week's cases. Please come up to the bench when your case is called."

The bailiff stood at parade-rest beside the judge.

"Timmons versus Timmons," the judge said.

Shapiro grabbed his briefcase and approached the bench.

So did the lady lawyer who had been painting her nails.

They both stood before the bench.

"Mr. Budding is my opponent in this case, Your Honor," Shapiro said. "Your order requires trial counsel to be present."

The judge looked to her friend.

"Ms. Ansel," the judge said, "care to respond?"

"I started working for Mr. Budding's firm this week. I'll be trying this case with him."

"Nothing wrong with that," the judge said. "What are the issues in this case?"

Ms. Ansel thumbed through her file.

"Alimony, child support and visitation," Shapiro said.

"Is the case ready for trial?" the judge asked.

"It is, Your Honor," Shapiro said. "It's been noticed for six months."

The judge leaned out over her desk and looked down.

"Are you implying, Counsel, that this court does not run its docket efficiently?"

Shapiro set his briefcase on a nearby table, so he could use both hands to speak.

"Of course not, Your Honor. It's just that my client has been extremely anxious to get the case tried and over with, and—"

"Who do you represent?"

"The husband."

"There's another slight problem," Ms. Ansel said.

"Yes," said the judge.

"Since I'm new on the case, I'll need a continuance of at least three months in order to bring myself up to speed."

Shapiro felt his blood pressure rising, hot. He wished he'd had a couple hours more sleep.

"That's ridiculous, Judge," Shapiro said. "Her boss is completely familiar with the case; there's no need for a continuance. There's been no proper motion filed under the rules. There's no—"

"That will be all, Mr. Shapiro. It's bad enough you come into my courtroom with your tie loose..."

Shapiro reached up to his neck. The collar had gotten too tight.

"...Now you're raising your voice, which I must say is quite resonate enough without your shouting."

Not since his first case after leaving Mel Forman's tutelage, had he been talked to like this by a judge.

"Your Honor, a continuance at this late stage is out of the question. My client will be devastated, financially and emotionally."

Judge Cindy Gievers looked at Ms. Ansel and smirked. "It's the system, sir. What can we as lawyers and judges do? The motion for continuance is granted."

"But Your Honor—"

"I've ruled, Counsel."

The bailiff came to attention and took a step toward Shapiro. The judge and Ms. Ansel looked at each other and smiled.

"Next case is Horner versus Central Electric Power."

Shapiro rode the elevator down alone. Some of the graffiti on the walls had been there since he'd begun practicing. Where were the lawyers he'd grown up with?

He left the elevator and stood for a moment in the courthouse lobby, hoping to see an old face, anybody he knew.

There was nobody.

Neal Shapiro was fifty years old, and the only lawyer from his law class to be found in the courthouse, still down in the trenches, banging out divorce cases. His contemporaries didn't do the actual fighting anymore. They sat up in their expensive offices and sunk putts on the carpet, while paying young women and men with law degrees to do the dirty work for them—young men and women who didn't know what it meant to be a lawyer any more than they knew what it was like to have unprotected sex. When had time passed him by? Had he done something wrong with his life?

Shapiro searched for an answer, each heavy step of the way back to the parking lot at the river flats. Had he finally hit the hot coals of what they call professional burnout?

"That'll be another five dollars," the parking lot attendant said, after Shapiro handed him the ticket.

"I've already paid enough."

"I'll call the police."

Shapiro tore the ticket into confetti and tossed it skyward. He walked beyond his car, all the way down to the riverbank, where there were benches. He sat and watched the dark flowing waters.

His friends from law school headed huge firms. They specialized, made big money. With Shapiro, it was a divorce here, a real estate closing or accident case there. Catch as catch can. How was he supposed to compete with the frosted-hair, fingernail polishers who had lunch with the mousy little judges?

He stood up, took off his coat and tie, and tossed them into the river. He watched as they floated away, just like the big case that had never come his way.

CHAPTER 2

Shapiro parked in front of his office building, a converted house on a block of northeast Seventh Avenue, in a residential area thirty minutes north of the courthouse. Before he entered through the smoked-glass storefront door, he ripped a flap of peeling paint from the outside wall that faced the street. The patch of naked concrete beneath looked better without the frayed ends sticking out. When had he last painted the little building? Instead of throwing the patch of clay-colored paint away, he took it with him inside—perhaps they could match it up at the paint store.

The client waiting room was the size of a small bathroom. It had two chairs and a padded bench that was built into the wall. All three of the seats were torn and had cotton stuffing showing. A low glass table was between the chairs, stacked two feet high with magazines that scanned three presidential administrations.

Shapiro stood there for a moment and looked at it all. When he first started practicing law, he made fun of the lawyers down on Charles Street—the ones whose offices looked like they'd been frozen in a time capsule, equipment and furniture thirty years old. What did the young lawyers think when they came to his office for a deposition?

He opened the glass pass-through window and hooked his arm around to the inner doorknob. He had put in a security buzzer-lock years before. One day he'd come back from court and found a young black man in his office, stuffing a dictation machine down his pants. It had been a toss-up who screamed louder, Shapiro or the thief.

Shapiro and his secretary had keys to the inner door, but they were never used.

"You're back early," Carol Emry said, from behind a low wooden partition that separated her desk from the aisle.

"Almost didn't come back."

"Who'd sign my paycheck?"

Shapiro stood over her.

"Who called?"

She pulled a pile of phone messages from the bill of a toy duck, which was on top of her computer monitor, and handed them to her boss.

Shapiro leafed through them.

"Mail come?" Shapiro asked.

"Your wife called."

"Any checks?"

"Why should today be special?"

"The statements we sent last week must be sitting at the bottom of our clients' trash baskets."

"Only if you're real lucky, then there might be a chance they'd get read. Flushed down the toilet is more likely."

Shapiro continued flipping through the messages, like he was looking through a deck of cards for the ace.

"Who's Manholm Reitz? Another stockbroker who thinks I've got money because I'm a lawyer?"

Carol gestured with her eyes. Her earphone was on, and she was typing dictation off the recorder. "They keep calling, who knows? So, when's the Timmons's case set?"

"It's not...continued because the judge felt like it."

"The client's going to dump you."

"He still owes me money, too. Why can't these judges understand that what they do reaches right into a lawyer's pocket? Didn't they ever practice law?"

Carol didn't answer, but went on typing.

"Bring my personal insurance file into my office, will you?" Shapiro said. "Coffee."

His office was the largest of three. It was nearest to the secretarial area. Across a narrow hall from him was the library-conference room. At the other end of the 1,200-square-foot building were two smaller lawyers' offices, both empty for the past three years. There was a bathroom and a storage room, which looked more like a legal trial museum, holding old exhibits, blowups, and even an old stove that was involved in the burning death of a mother and two small children. The State Fire Marshall found no liability, no case.

Once in a while, Shapiro would go in there and stare at what could have been.

Shapiro threw his briefcase on the sofa against the wall. He sat at his desk, sorting the phone messages in stacks of priority. He crumpled and tossed the one from the stockbroker.

Carol came in with a brown expandable file, filled with smaller manilla folders, and a cup of coffee.

"What's with your insurance all of a sudden, Nick?"

"Need to see what I've got."

"You don't know?"

"Sometimes I pay the premiums; sometimes I

don't. I could have disability coverage, then again...."

Carol stood by Shapiro's side. She placed the file on the desk. "Tell me what you're looking for," she said. "I'll find it."

She had put on a few pounds over the years, but her legs still looked tight, sexy in her pants. There was a time when Shapiro would run his hand up the back of her legs when Carol was showing him a file. She'd let him, liked it. They did more, but that was when she was married. Now that she was divorced, it was too risky.

"I'll get what I need," Shapiro said. "Hold my calls for a while."

Carol backed off a step.

"Everything all right, Nick?"

"Right as cold vodka and herring."

She raised her hand to reach for him, but the man who had once been her lover was too busy looking through the files.

How had it been possible to accumulate such clutter?

Shapiro was tossing out receipts for payments on policies that had been canceled more than ten years before. He took from the files what appeared to be policies that were still in effect. He had more coverage on his fax machine than he did on his own life. After age forty-five, the premiums became impossible to pay. There was only a five thousand dollar term policy of life insurance in force.

He walked across the hall to the library and brought back to his office a law book on insurance. Before he opened it, he stared at the pictures of his wife and children on the desk. Then he opened the book to the section on incontestability clauses. Suicide, it seemed, was covered if it was committed more than two years after the effective date of the policy.

Shapiro brought the file back out to Carol.

"Find what you were looking for?" she said.

"Unfortunately."

"That bad, huh?"

"I wouldn't have the guts to kill myself, anyhow."

"Nick!"

"It's over, the whole thing."

"What did you have for lunch?"

"I took a good look at myself this morning, Carol. I'm a relic of the past, too stupid, or scared, to have made my move when I should have. Now I'm looking at life's caboose speed down the tracks."

Carol got up from her desk and closed the blinds to the window that overlooked the back parking lot. She locked the office door.

"You're still handsome, Nick, better looking than before, I think."

She put her arms around him and laid her head on his shoulder. He smelled her perfume.

"It wouldn't be any good, you know," he said. "It's been too long."

"I don't care—I miss what we had."

They kissed. It wasn't the same. Only a spark arced across Neal Shapiro's heart.

But at least it told him he was still alive.

CHAPTER 3

Shapiro stepped into the kitchen of his house.

"Where are the kids?"

"Oh, Neal, you frightened me."

"Nick."

"I still can't get used to calling you that. You don't look like a 'Nick'."

"Indulge me. Go ahead, say it. Nick."

"Neal." Marilee Shapiro smiled and shook her head. "You always seem more tired than when we were first married, Neal."

"And your tits are a lot bigger."

"You like that, don't you?"

Nick grabbed his wife around the waist, pulled her into him and felt her up.

"Two kids and nature saved me four thousand dollars for the boob job."

"Men like women with big boobs."

"I thought we already established that—but I like only yours." He let go of her waist. "Had a rough day. I'll make a drink. Want one?"

"A double."

Nick went into the family room, behind the bar, and poured out two straight scotches, no ice. He came back into the kitchen and sat.

"You didn't work out tonight," Marilee said. She

was at the stove, her back to Nick.

"Wanted to see the kids—before they were too busy with the mall, or the movies, wherever else they disappear to by the time I get home."

"All of a sudden you want to see the kids when you get home from work?"

"Today's different."

Marilee stirred the tomato sauce, then lifted the wooden spoon and tasted.

"What's so different? You should've worked out, maybe get rid of some of that stress. The kids aren't home."

Nick took a swallow of his scotch. He swirled the golden-brown liquid around in the glass, watching it ebb and flow. Then he looked up at his wife.

"Life makes no sense."

"I guess you had another bad day."

"It's as if my world has become a big bathtub—and someone pulled the plug."

Marilee turned to face him.

"You're not in trouble with the bar, are you?"

"Only with my soul. I think it's dead."

Nick finished his drink in one big gulp.

His wife put the burner on low and sat with him at the table. "Neal, are you all right?"

"I thought about killing myself today. Checked the insurance policy to see what it would leave you and the kids."

She grabbed Nick's hand. "How much was it?"

"Everything I've ever done in my life—college, the army, law school, all the years spent straining to earn a living—none of it has any meaning. It's as if I've been running in a big circle, chasing my own tail, always worrying about everything, for no purpose or reason at all."

"I had no idea you—"

"I can't go on like this, Marilee. The very thought of practicing penny-ante law until I'm old enough to collect social security makes me want to curl up into a ball—and stop breathing."

"It puts the bread on our table."

"Too late...too late."

"We need to get away, Neal. A real vacation this time—Europe, Spain. Someplace where we can come home refreshed."

Nick got up and made another drink. He came back to the kitchen.

Marilee took the glass from his hand. He took it back. "Maybe you need to see a psychiatrist, Neal."

Five years ago he would have been insulted at what she'd said; maybe even said some things back to her he'd have regretted in the morning.

"How's a shrink going to chop me out of this block of ice I've been frozen into? No doctor can give me the success that's turned its back on me— no matter how good the drugs he prescribes."

Marilee got up and went to the counter. She started to boil water in a big metal pot, then took down a package of noodles from the cupboard and poured in the spaghetti.

Nick took his first tension-free breath of the day. The scotch was working.

The evening newspaper lay open on the kitchen table. He began to read the local section, an article about a two-month-old baby who had been killed when a van rear-ended the car he was riding in on the interstate. A car in front had stalled and the parents had stopped in time, but the van that rear-ended them had been speeding.

"Did you read the paper?" Nick said.

"It's always the same old crap."

"There's an article about a baby that was killed on I-51."

Marilee shrugged her shoulders.

"It's got to be the worst thing a parent could ever go through," Nick said, "losing a child. The thought of Debbie getting her license makes my blood run cold. Those poor people."

Nick finished his scotch. "Poor baby never even had a chance at life."

Marilee continued to mix the spaghetti.

"Why couldn't I ever get a case like that?" Nick asked. "There's only a handful of lawyers around town who get the big ones. Wonder if they ever care about the families—or is it just the money?"

"Why torture yourself by dreaming?" Marilee said.

"Even if a case like that came my way, I wouldn't be able to finance it. Do you know how much a big case costs to bring to trial? A hundred thousand or more. Expert witnesses, product models, mockups. It's why run-of-the-mill lawyers like me refer the good cases out, even if we get lucky enough to land one. Only the big boys can pay for it. At least, we'd get a referral fee."

"I thought it was because of the specialty. A real estate lawyer couldn't handle a death case."

"No, but I could. I've got more trial experience than most of those snot noses who're making millions. With all the little cases I've beat my brains out for, just once I'd like to take a shot at the big time. I could do it."

"In the meantime, we've got to pay the mortgage and the electric bill. There's college to think about."

Nick used the tip of a knife and began to cut the article from the newspaper. The knife slipped and cut the article in half. He gave up.

"And," Marilee said, "I don't ever want to hear you talk about...killing yourself again. My father

used to talk like that, and then he had a stroke."
She continued to mumble under her breath. The
front door opened, then slammed shut. Within
seconds, Debbie Shapiro walked into the kitchen.
Her sun-colored golden hair bounced with each
step.

"Hi, Mom," she said, "what's going on?" She
did a double take. "Daddy? What are you doing
here?"

"I live here."

Debbie giggled, half-girl, half-woman.

"I mean, I'm not used to seeing you home at
this time."

She gave her father a peck on the cheek.

Nick was about to say something to his daughter. He looked at his wife first. Marilee held her
finger across her lips.

Nick said, "I came home early to see you and
Tommy."

"Lame."

The front door opened and closed again.
Tommy ran into the kitchen.

"Dad, Dad! I hit a home run today. Over the
fence on the fly. The wind was at our backs, but
still—"

Come here, you two," Nick said.

He put his arms around his children. What
would they do without him? Probably grow into
fine human beings. *What would he do without
them?*

"Let's all make a pact," Nick said. "Every Thursday evening from now on we all have dinner *together*, here at home. Everyone helps cook, and
we all clean up. What do you think?"

"Do I get a car when I get my licence?" Debbie
asked.

"No conditions here," Nick said. "I'm serious."

"So am I," his daughter said.

"We'll see about the car."

"It's a thought," Marilee said.

"Thursday is fairy day," Tommy said.

Nick and the kids stood in a circle, like a football huddle, arms intertwined.

"Tinkerbell," Nick said.

"Who's that?" Tommy asked.

"A fairy I used to know."

CHAPTER 4

Shapiro was barely able to pull himself out of bed. Marilee was already off to work and the kids were at school by the time he finally had the courage to open his eyes and turn on the clock radio. Nine-thirty. A shower, shave, and he was in his car headed to the office.

"The phone's been ringing for an hour already," Carol said.

"That's what you get paid for," Shapiro said. "To answer it."

She handed him phone messages.

"Do you have any idea how much business you're losing by coming in so late?"

"Big deal. A three hundred dollar divorce here, or a two hundred dollar closing there? I'll call them all back. Coffee."

Shapiro sat behind his desk, the same one he'd had since the day he left Mel Forman's office. How much money had passed across the top of it in all that time? Not enough, that was for certain. He tossed the phone messages in the trash basket next to him.

Carol came in and set the steaming styrofoam cup on the desk.

"Nick, why don't you place an ad in *Preview*,

rent out the other offices to a couple of young lawyers, get some action going around here."

He took a sip of the coffee. Too hot.

"Ouch, goddammit!" He touched the tip of his tongue. "What for?"

"Maybe it'll help get *you* going."

"I'm going all right, right down the crapper."

"You've got an eleven-thirty at the branch courthouse. Uncontested divorce before Judge Hexter."

"Call the client, cancel. I'm not up for it."

"Nick...that's a major pain in the ass and you know it."

"Just do it. I can't face Hexter today. If one *i* isn't dotted, he ridicules the attorneys in front of everybody...doesn't let up either."

"He doesn't ridicule you. You both go back too far...didn't you hush up his wife's DUI?"

"I just hate to see how ornery he is on the bench with everyone else. It makes *me* feel uneasy."

"The case'll come up again in two weeks."

"Cancel."

"Fine."

"And shut the door on your way out."

"Have a fight with your wife this morning?"

"I'm just—"

"Burned out?"

Nick sat there.

"I know what it is, and I know what can cure it. You and me should hop in the sack with each other once in a while. It'll change your outlook on things."

Shapiro tapped the picture of his wife with a pencil eraser.

"What if I told you I wasn't interested in sex anymore."

"I'd personally pay for the shrink."

"We'll talk about it later. I've got some things I need to catch up on. Busy out there?"

"Nuts."

"I'll buzz you for some dictation in a while."

"That's what I was hoping you'd do to me right now...buzz me."

Shapiro flipped the pencil at her.

Carol closed the door in time to avoid the pencil, blocking it, and leaving him by himself, the way he wanted to be.

On the right side of Shapiro's big desk was a foot-high stack of old *Newsweeks*, bar journals, and *Previews*. None had been read. To the side of those were unpaid bills, some so late that second and third notices were included.

The left side of the desk housed two columns of unopened mail and a large array of client files that needed work.

Shapiro made a circle of his arms and pushed outward, spreading it all out, so that a clear space was left on the desktop in front of him.

He thumbed through the magazines, took out a month-old *Sports Illustrated* and opened it. He skipped all the basketball articles—he didn't like the reverse exploitation of black players by white owners and fans—and began reading a spoof on baseball strikes. What if a new season were to start and the fans didn't come? Shapiro had never protested anything in his life, but he'd carry a placard for that one.

He opened the window blinds next to his chair and looked out at the traffic on Seventh Avenue. Before the county widened it to hook up with the interstate as the main east-west connector to busy 170th Street, it had been a sleepy, little residential road. The county commission changed the zoning on the one-mile stretch, which accounted for many of the houses being converted into small office buildings.

How exciting that had been: to build the office—Shapiro's only real investment. But now that the neighborhood had changed, property values had dropped. He couldn't sell the building for what he had put into it fifteen years before. Now he was doomed to stay there for as long as he continued to practice law.

The cars raced by in both directions. Once, about two years ago, an old lady had lost control of her vehicle in front of the office. It had hit a grass berm on the corner and went airborne, twisting in flight as it careened forward. Shapiro had been staring out the window then, too. The car was heading right for him. He didn't move, just watched it come at him as if he accepted it somehow. When the end was apparent, the car hit the sturdy trunk of a star-apple tree and came crashing to the sidewalk, up-side-down. Miraculously, the old lady was unharmed. How sudden a life could be blotted out.

He'd lived long enough.

Carol opened the office door, holding her mug of steaming coffee. Shapiro jumped, his hand banging the blind, making a harp sound.

"Didn't meant to frighten you," Carol said.

"You should knock first."

"You were daydreaming again."

Carol wore a blue, knee-length dress with red, high-heel shoes. Her auburn-dyed hair was professionally done, and she wore makeup. It usually meant clients were coming. She set her coffee on the desk. It gave her a view of her boss's wastepaper basket.

"You threw the phone messages away. Why

bother to spend money on a yellow page ad?"

She bent over and picked up the slips from the trash, closed the magazine shut, and put them all on the desk.

"I'm not trying to tell you how to run your business," Carol continued, "but if you don't work, I don't get paid. I could go downtown for another hundred bucks a week you know—then you'd really have something to get depressed about."

Carol picked up her coffee and closed the door behind her.

Shapiro pushed the messages aside and opened the magazine again. But when he couldn't find anything interesting, he spread out the six phone messages in front of him.

One was from a lawbook salesman; another was from the probate clerk. He shoved those out of the way, up to the left of the desktop. Divorce...divorce...child support...King Albert Alonso, accident.

What kind of a name was that? And why didn't Carol take more detailed messages about the calls? That way he didn't have to return the call if it was just another fender bender, or a fight over ashtrays and who gets to keep the dog.

He dialed King Albert's number. Maybe it was a European nobleman who fell off his horse while in town for the polo match. Shapiro could use a good laugh.

"Hello."

"Is there a King Albert Alonso there?"

"Just a minute," a child's voice said. "I get him...Daddy, there's a white man on the phone."

The man's voice was slow, hoarse.

"This is King Albert."

"My name's Neal Shapiro, an attorney you called earlier?"

"Yes, Mr. Shapiro. My cousin, Norman Brown, told me to call you...say you a real good attorney."

"Norman Brown—"

"You help him on a problem he have with his house—then got him some money back from the guy who cheat him when he sold the lawn business to him."

"How long ago was that?"

"Three, four years. Norman say you don't even charge him. He give you a bottle of vodka."

Shapiro folded the phone message into a paper airplane and sailed it across the room. Another freebie coming right up. "I don't remember your cousin...and I'm not inter—"

King Albert broke down.

"They killed my baby boy, Mr. Shapiro."

"Killed...a baby?"

"Never even laid down skid marks, baby crushed in the backseat—two months old—"

"When did this happen?"

"Yesterday. On I-51, just past downtown."

"Was there an article about it in last night's paper?"

"Someone said so."

Shapiro held the phone to his chest and took in a deep breath. It was the case he had read about in his kitchen, with Marilee.

"I can't tell you how sorry I am about this, Mr. Alonso. My wife and I thought it was so tragic."

"Norman said you were a good man."

Shapiro had gotten called on cases like this before. But each time something was wrong: an uninsured at-fault driver, alcohol contributing to the accident, one of the big boys downtown poaching the case before it reached fruition—something, anything to blot out the big fee.

"I know you may not want to talk about the

details right now, Mr. Alonso—"

"It's O.K."

"How did the accident happen?"

"We was going south on I-51...."

"Who was in the car?"

"My wife and me. The baby, Calvin, was in the back seat."

"In an infant seat?"

"Yes."

Shapiro wrote on a yellow pad and made a check mark.

"Go on."

"We was taking the baby to the doctor."

"Was he all right?"

"Fine, a routine checkup with the pediatrician. A car was stalled right there on the expressway. I stopped in time. A van behind crashed into us...."

King Albert had to stop for a moment. There was the snapping of a handkerchief, sniffling, and wiping.

"Mr. Alonso—"

"You call me King Albert; we about the same age."

"What kind of vehicles were they?"

"The one in front was a new 4x4."

Shapiro made another check mark. New cars always had insurance. But how much?

"The van was old, but had a lot of tools in it. The guy was a plumber, worked for a company. He was laughing when the police were talking to him."

One more check. If the driver was in the course and scope of his employment, there'd be a big liability policy. Laughing? Maybe he was drunk, which would mean punitive damages.

"There something else," King Albert said. "The highway patrolman say the safety buckle on the infant seat broke off."

Another check, big and bold.

"What kind of car were you driving?"

"'88 Ibis, four-door."

"Where is it now?"

"Highway patrol towed what was left of it, don't know for sure."

"I'll need to have an expert examine the car...."

Shapiro stopped himself before he got too far. The expense. What was he getting into? He should quit right there and refer the case out.

"There are a lot of other lawyers in this town, King Albert. Once I get involved, I want to know that you and I will see this thing through to the end, together."

"Somehow, I feel like I already know you, Mr. Shapiro. I'll do whatever you say."

"Then tell me...."

The mattress of the king-sized bed hadn't been turned for years. Indentations of Shapiro and his wife, Marilee, could be seen on their respective sides.

Shapiro stripped the bed, raised the huge mattress and flipped it.

The whoosh of air blew up Marilee's negligee, exposing her thighs. She pulled the hem down.

"Why do this all of a sudden?" she asked, standing next to the bed. "And at this hour?"

"It's time."

Shapiro maneuvered the mattress into place with his knees and began replacing the sheets.

"Is it just a coincidence—a cosmic fluke—or is there some other reason why King Albert called me to take the case?"

She helped her husband with the sheets.

"A cosmic fluke."

Shapiro fluffed up the pillows against the head-board and plopped down on his side of the bed.

"Ahhh...it feels like brand new."

Marilee rolled over on top of him.

"What about me, Nick? You haven't turned me over in years, either."

"Sure I have. Hey, you called me Nick."

Marilee cuddled in close.

"But not with the same passion."

"Thought I'd lost the desire for everything that was good in life...now this case has come my way."

"You almost seem apologetic about it."

"I don't know if I can handle it. For starters, I don't have a spare hundred thousand sitting around to finance it."

"You could always get the money from Freddy if you needed it...maybe business will pick up and you won't need Freddy."

"Freddy...he's my brother and he loves me, but I don't like taking advantage. If I lost the case, I'd never be able to pay him back. There are just too many things that need to fall into place to make this work. It might be easier to refer the case to a big boy downtown, just take the referral fee."

"Maybe this is your time in the sun, Nick—you know, like those insects that lie dormant most of their lives, then blossom out in May and control the insect world."

"So you think I'm a bug."

Marilee rubbed the patch of hair on Nick's chest.

"Where's the old confidence you had when you used to free innocent men from prison, or win custody away from a drug-addicted mother?"

"I've lost that, too."

"It's still there."

"I know, dormant, like the insects."

"Nick, make love to me like you used to, hard; kiss me while we do it."

He felt Marilee's silk gown rise up on her legs and felt the old heat.

Where *had* his soul been hiding all this time?

CHAPTER 5

Attorney Neal Shapiro had never been in this part of town before.

It was a vast residential area out behind the old pro-football stadium, still used for high school games, but not much more. All the houses looked the same, wooden boxes fit more for storage sheds than human shelter. Most street numbers had long since fallen off the houses, or had been stolen by vandals.

Shapiro checked King Albert Alonso's address, which he had scrawled on the yellow pad, one more time.

Everywhere, throngs of children roamed the streets, stopping to eyeball the only white person within ten square blocks. Shapiro didn't stop the car to ask for help.

At the end of a block of houses, where there were more paint chips on the grassless yards than on the walls, there was a tidy little brown house with freshly painted, maroon trim. The street numbers matched Shapiro's notes.

He pulled into the driveway, homemade with parallel flagstones, behind a ten-year-old Japanese car.

There were a dozen sets of eyes on him from

across the street. He walked up the sidewalk to the house.

The doorbell worked.

A black man, well under six feet and with a smooth, shining face came to the screen door.

"You must be Mr. Shapiro."

"How did you guess?"

"You the only one in the neighborhood holding a briefcase."

King Albert opened the door.

Shapiro entered.

A large metal fan on a stand was in a corner blowing warm air across the room. Heavy curtains swayed at the window's sides. There weren't enough lights.

"Have a seat, Mr. Shapiro," King Albert said.

Shapiro sat on a sofa that had white doilies on the armrests. Opposite him were two reupholstered, cushioned chairs. High up on one wall was a large painting of a black Jesus. A two-foot-long, golden metal crucifix was on the other wall, facing Jesus' picture. A console TV, the old kind with doors that closed over the screen, was turned on. The picture was all wavy, with bent lines and no sound.

King Albert noticed Shapiro looking at it.

"We don't get good reception around here," he said. "Even with a roof antenna, something about the metal in the stadium blocking the signals."

"No cable?"

"Can't afford it."

King Albert wore a pair of jeans that had blue and red paint stains all over the legs. His white tee-shirt was gritty, as if he had just been working. It fit tight, exposing a small potbelly that looked out of place on his otherwise muscular body.

He sat opposite Shapiro.

A young woman came in the room from the adjoining kitchen.

Shapiro stood.

"This my daughter, Wanda," King Albert said.

"I thought she was your—"

"She got a scholarship to Wisconsin next year, fast-pitch softball."

Wanda tried to smile, but couldn't.

The bead strings that separated the kitchen from the living room spread open. A woman, with two small boys at her knees, entered. She sat in the chair next to King Albert, saying nothing.

Wanda sat on the arm of the chair, next to her mother. The boys, on the other arm, were trying to put their arms around her.

"This my wife, Muriel," King Albert said. "She don't say much since the accident. Got banged up pretty good herself...flying glass.

Shapiro laid the briefcase on his lap, the legal pad on top of that. "Would it be better if we spoke alone?"

"She's a strong woman; we can talk."

Shapiro noticed that Muriel was holding a fuzzy, blue baby blanket. She sniffed it occasionally. It had belonged to Calvin.

"I'll know the details a lot better after I get the homicide report," Shapiro said. "For now, there are a few things I need to find out."

King Albert nodded.

"Where was the baby sitting in the car?"

"Calvin in the backseat, behind me. Muriel in the back too, next to him."

"Was the infant seat strapped in by the car's safety belt?"

Muriel lowered the blanket from her cheek.

"Yes, it was," she said. Her voice was weak, but certain. "Surely was."

Shapiro wrote.

"Other than the cuts and bruises on your legs and arms, did either of you receive any injuries?"

Muriel crossed herself.

"Praise the Lord...we was spared. But our little baby!" She broke down.

King Albert and Wanda joined her in loud sobs.

"Our baby dead!" King Albert's voice was deep now, sounding like a preacher in despair.

The twins looked confused.

Shapiro opened the briefcase and put his notes inside. It would be no use to continue the questioning. He could supplement the investigative reports with their statements later.

He took the retainer agreement and release forms from the case. But how could he talk business now? The crying had become so intense that even Shapiro's eyes welled with tears. After a full minute, the sobs slowed to erratic breathing. Then it was calm.

"I'll be handling the case on a contingency fee basis: I get paid only out of the monies I recover for you by trial or settlement."

"How much you take?" King Albert said.

"Forty percent, the standard rate. All costs that I advance, such as filing fees, court reporter fees, expert witness fees, get reimbursed to me out off the top of the settlement proceeds. The rest is yours."

Muriel rubbed the blanket between her thumb and forefinger, then said in a far-off voice, "All the money in God's green world ain't gonna bring my baby Calvin back."

"Amen," Wanda said.

"How much my baby's life worth, Mr. Shapiro?" King Albert said.

Shapiro always hated that question. Quote too

little and they think you're not a good lawyer; too much, and you're setting yourself up for a malpractice action down the road if you didn't get that amount.

"I always come up with that number the night before my closing argument to the jury," Shapiro said.

"Ballpark," King Albert said.

"A dozen things could affect it: liability problems, contributory negligence, much more."

King Albert thought for a moment. "There a difference between money for a white baby and money for a black baby?" Shapiro squirmed a little.

"Hate to say it, but it depends on who's on the jury."

"Then I'll leave it all in your hands, Mr. Shapiro."

Why did he have to say that?

Shapiro put the retainer contract on the coffee table, turned it up-side-down, and pointed with his pen.

"Now if you'll both sign here and here."

The signatures of King Albert and Muriel Alonso sparkled out from the contract like gold leaf. Shapiro held the paper in front of him, and read it as if it were one of the tablets from Mt. Sinai, black fire on white fire.

It was the biggest case he had ever signed up.

"I'll walk you out to the car," King Albert said.

Shapiro said his goodbyes to the family.

Outside on the driveway, the two men stood and looked at each other.

"I feel like I know you from some place," King Albert said.

Shapiro set his briefcase on the hood of his car. "I was about to say the same thing about you."

He glanced over at the towering brick stadium walls in the distance. "I've never been on this side of the ballpark."

"I never been on your side."

They each forced a laugh.

King Albert said, "The funeral home wants nine hundred dollars to take care of Calvin. Another seven hundred dollars later to put him in the ground. I been laid off two weeks now."

There was silence while Shapiro tried to absorb this.

Was this just the beginning, the touch that would be "paid back" at the end of the case? He'd heard of lawyers who had to advance tens of thousands to clients while a big case was pending. Some even paid their mother-in-law's living expenses. A higher bidder was always waiting in the wings to steal the good cases.

But King Albert was asking nothing for himself, only to bury his son.

"Come by my office tomorrow morning, around eleven," Shapiro said. "I'll have a check for you."

King Albert put his arms around Shapiro.

"God bless you, Mr. Shapiro."

God bless you, King Albert.

CHAPTER 6

Nick Shapiro opened the buzzer-lock inner office door. The buzzer no longer worked.

His secretary, Carol Emry, looked up from her computer screen.

"It must have gone well with King Albert," she said, "you're not complaining."

"I'm worried."

"The biggest case of your life just landed in your lap, and you're worried? About what, how to spend all the money?"

Nick shook his head. "How to get the money to finance the case, for starters."

"I've heard of lawyers mortgaging their houses, their mother's houses too, in order to pay for a case like this one."

"I'm scared."

"You?"

"Just can't get it in my mind that I'm finally going to be on the same field with the big boys. They'll paper us to death—pleadings, motions, depositions. Think of the hearings. There'll be no time to work on anything else to make money— and they know it with a guy like me, revel in it."

"If it's going to bug you that much, refer the case out to Bobby Hawkins. I'm sure he could use another couple million bucks. You'd get your split, and that would be the comfortable end of it."

Nick sat on the edge of Carol's desk, rubbing his thighs up and down. "I'd be giving away three-quarters of the fee."

Carol stood and faced Nick. She put her hands on his head and squeezed his skull, hard.

"There's supposed to be a brain inside there. You've got to make a decision, Nick. Either refer the case or go for it full blast."

"I'm just a one-man firm—"

"Look around at this office. We've both turned into dinosaurs. When young lawyers come here for a deposition, they ask me if that thing on my desk is really a computer. Is that the way you want to go on, until you really are extinct?"

Nick spoke to the far wall. "If the case was won, a referral fee would be in the six figures—more money than I've ever seen at once."

"And where would that leave you? You pay for college, weddings, a few lavish vacations, a fancy car; then it's gone. Don't you want to set yourself up for life? And me, too, for that matter? I deserve it after putting up with you all these years."

Nick stood, took Carol by the shoulders, stared at her lips and chest and remembered how she looked naked. He took a deep breath, then let her go.

"I'd live the life of a wealthy man—or finish myself off in the attempt."

"You're a good lawyer, Nick. I know what you can do in the courtroom. You can win it on your own."

"Win, the future's clear. Lose...."

"You've got the guts, Nick."

"Or I could sell hot dogs downtown from a pushcart."

"Decide, Nick."
"I can win this case on my own."
"Is that the plan, Nick?"
He didn't answer.

CHAPTER 7

Carol Emry sat in one of the cushy chairs in front of Nick's desk, her long legs crossed, steno pad at the ready.

"Do the standard letters to County Memorial," Nick said. "Baby's medical records and the parents'. I want the highway patrol, homicide and medical examiner reports. The police took photos at the scene, I want them all, color blowups, also the autopsy photos of the baby. What time is Jerry Dockett going to be here?"

Carol looked at her watch. "Noon. Was that all one sentence?"

"Is Dockett still on the wagon?"

Carol shifted in her seat.

"I wouldn't know."

Nick stared at her. She knew all right. She would have married Dockett after her divorce, except for the booze. He wasn't a mean drunk, just got too honest when he was high. Booze or not, Dockett was the best personal-injury private investigator in town—when the lawyers could get him to work.

"And I want an ad in the *Preview* for the empty offices," Nick said, "something short but catchy."

"You mean cheap."

Nick smiled. "How about 'sole practitioner seeks two energetic associates to share space, referrals.'"

"That'll get you two kids right out of law school. Maybe you should go for more experience, especially if you're going to get them involved in the Alonso case."

"Anybody with experience is going to want to be paid."

"A reasonable request for a lawyer."

"Let them do it the way I did it: earn their own way. Besides, I'd be picking up all the overhead. Run the ad for a week; let's see who we get."

Carol scribbled in shorthand.

Nick fanned through his Rolodex twice before looking up at her.

"What was the name of that expert we used on the Fineberg Lemon Law case? The guy was great. Defense lawyers couldn't shake him an inch on cross."

"David Halgers."

"How can you remember things like that? It was, what, eight years ago?"

"Six—and the Alzheimer's hasn't set in on *me* yet."

"Not funny. If my brain goes, so does your job. Get his number for me, will you?"

Carol wrote.

"That should cover it until Dockett gets here," Nick said.

The front doorbell rang; the chime malfunctioned so the dong sounded like two wooden sticks pounding together in a jungle call.

"I'll be right back," Carol said.

She answered the front door, then returned.

"There's a walk-in at the door, a woman."

"Christ, now? Tell her to leave. Walk-ins are

nothing but trouble, and they have no money."

"She looks really depressed."

"That's even worse."

"See her, Nick. She's been crying."

Nick stood and straightened his tie.

"Why is it you can always get me to do what I don't want to do?"

"Not always, Nick, not lately."

Nick frowned. "What's it about?"

"She wouldn't tell me."

"All right, I'll see her. But the minute Dockett gets here, you buzz me, got it?"

Carol returned to her word processor in the central secretarial area. From there she had a view of the inner door that led to the small reception room.

Nick opened the door fast, not looking as he spoke.

"My name's Neal Shapiro. I'm an attorney; what can I help you with?"

Nick's tone was cold, but after he'd greeted her like that, he wished he hadn't. The woman, not much over thirty, and with a flowing mountain of blond hair, had puffy, red cheeks and globs of mascara running down over one eye.

"I don't live far from here," she said, her voice still shaky, "...driven past your office for years...I was wondering if you could see me for a moment."

Years ago someone came in off the street, laid a bloody knife on Nick's desk, and told him he'd just stabbed a guy. "What is this about?"

"I can't live with my husband anymore. I think I want a divorce."

More handholding, and no money. Nick turned to look at Carol.

She nodded with her head toward his office.

"Would you like to come in...?"

"Barbara Irati." The woman tried to force a smile.

"It's this way, here on the left. Have a seat."

Nick closed his door.

They both sat.

"You don't look like an 'Irati.' What kind of a name is that, Arab?"

"Persian. My husband's from Iran."

Another American girl married to an Iranian. They beat their women, kidnapped their children, and hated people named Shapiro. But, worst of all, they were convenience store night clerks with no money to pay their wives' lawyers.

"How long have you been married to him?"

"Eight years. We have a daughter who's six."

The purse opened almost automatically. Out came a wad of tissue to soak up the tears.

"My husband's been defrauding the IRS and I don't want to be part of it any longer. I don't want to go to prison with him, my daughter needs me."

Another bloody knife? But what's this about the IRS? Nick thought.

"What type of business is your husband in?"

"Mexican floor tiles."

"One of those franchises?"

"His own place, deals mainly in cash. That's the problem."

"Cash is a problem?"

"He doesn't report it—agents are snooping around, asking questions. I've signed joint tax returns with him!"

"Sounds like you need a good CPA, not a divorce lawyer."

"I took $142,000 out of a shoebox in our closet before I left him. I'm staying at a motel right now."

Nick's eyes widened. No sense in getting too excited, yet. She could be a flake.

"Hmmm. Any violence, does he beat you?"

"Not physically, mentally he does. Tortures me with his words, his insane accusations."

"Sometimes that can be worse than a punch in the nose. You'll need a restraining order. If he comes around you, the police will arrest him on the spot."

"I've got plane tickets." She held them up from her purse. "Taking my daughter to Indiana. We'll stay with my aunt while you get the papers ready. I don't want to be here when he gets them."

"A case like this can get expensive. I'd need a seventy-five hundred dollar retainer in advance. When that gets used up at my hourly rate of two hundred dollars, I'll need more."

Mrs. Irati took a brown envelope from her purse and counted out seventy-five hundred dollar bills with the speed of a bank teller.

"Can you start right away?" she said.

She put the money in a pile and pushed it to the center of Nick's desk.

He hesitated for a moment, as if in prayer. Nick scooped up the money and put it in his drawer.

"Under no circumstances do you give your husband any information of your exact whereabouts. I need to see a judge about that restraining order first."

"What's going to happen, Mr. Shapiro?"

"You're going to live a long happy life, and so is your daughter—without being abused. I'll get you the house, alimony, child support, a piece of his business."

Mrs. Irati tried to smile.

"I don't want anything from him. Just out, safe."

"Everyone says that in your state of mind. Don't worry about a thing; leave it all to me. I've handled hundreds of these cases and they all turn out the same."

The tears started again, heavier this time.

"He's threatened to take my kid back to Iran with him."

"That's another thing they all say. Back to Iran, back to Texas. Bastards. They try to scare women into staying with them. I'll have the judge confiscate his passport. Your daughter's not going anywhere you don't want her to go."

"You can do that for me?"

"I'm just getting warmed up."

Within thirty seconds after Barbara Irati had left, Carol came into her boss's office.

"Mind telling me what *that* was all about?"

"Oh, not much. Just the best damn divorce case we've had in the office in the past five years. You wouldn't believe the things Mexican tiles can buy. Land in Florida, Swiss bank accounts, bundles of cash in safes. This girl was smart; she at least took a chunk of it for herself before she got out. It's called divorce planning."

"There's something sad about her face."

"She's going through a divorce."

"No, it's more...like she's frightened about something."

Shapiro reached into his drawer, pulled out a hundred dollar bill and gave it to Carol.

"We're all scared of something."

"What's this for?" Carol asked.

"Because you made me see her. I would have just blown her off."

"God, if only I was married to you, Nick. You know how to take care of a woman."

Carol folded the bill, then turned it over in her hand.

"Oh, I almost forgot," she said. "Jerry Dockett's here."

"I told you to buzz me."
"Complaining?"
Shapiro cracked a big smile.
"Shoot me if I do."

CHAPTER 8

His eyes were puffy, and the red blotches that previously had covered only the points of his cheeks were now all over his face, mostly the nose. But Jerry Dockett seemed otherwise fit and sober.

"Long time, no get paycheck. How you been, Nick?" Dockett asked.

Dockett sat in the same chair Barbara Irati had just vacated.

"Been working, Jerry?" Shapiro said.

"Here and there. I know you haven't, personal injury at least. It's been a couple years since I did a case for you."

"I think my secretary's still got the hots for you."

"She likes the bulges in men's pants."

Shapiro unloosened his tie and rolled up his left sleeve.

"I just don't want it to get in the way of things, if you know what I mean."

"I haven't laid a glove on her in months, I swear...so what's this all about?"

"Listen, Jerry. I've just signed up the biggest case of my career, a dead baby out on I-51."

"Rear-ended by a van?"

"Don't tell me my friends who swim with the sharks have already gotten to you on this one?"

"Not a chance, Nick. Read it in the paper. Heard it on my police scanner, too. But I was in no condition to go out and cap it."

"Well, you've got it now."

The private investigator put his hands together and leaned forward onto the desk on massive arms.

"You're not going to refer it out?"

"I'm keeping this one, Jerry."

"You know what you're getting yourself into?"

"That's one of the reasons you're here. I need help from the best."

Dockett sat back in his chair.

"I get fifty bucks an hour now, plus expenses and mileage. Nick, you sure you can afford to do this? And I mean that in more ways than one."

Nick moved the yellow pad to the center of the desk.

"Just tell me where the hell we start."

Dockett took a small notebook from his shirt pocket. The ballpoint pen seemed lost in his beefy hand.

"I'll need details of the accident: names, dates, what police departments were involved. You've probably asked Carol to order all the reports by mail—it'll take weeks that way. I'll hand walk them through. It will be only hours instead. In my business, we trade on favors, and I'm owed plenty."

While Dockett was a cop on the force, he'd stumbled onto a multilevel drug sting gone bad. Automatic weapons were bursting all over a residential intersection when he was coming home from his bowling night. Two FBI agents and three local cops were already down and hurt badly when he opened up with a sawed-off shotgun he'd forgotten to give back to the property room. When it was over, five bad guys were dead and a sixth wounded. Instead of getting a medal, Dockett was kicked off the force for using an illegal weapon. But his brothers in blue never forgot.

Shapiro spent the next thirty minutes going over the facts with Dockett. He gave the investigator photocopies of his notes to make it easier. He made sure to make the copies himself while Dockett stayed in the office. He didn't want Carol— or her perfume—to upset the balance.

Dockett finished reading the notes, then looked up at Nick from under thick eyebrows.

"If my hunch is right, a Corporal Henning Hutchins will be the highway patrol honcho on this one. He's thorough, right down to the thickness of the rubber laid down by the skid marks."

"You know him?" Shapiro said.

"Enough to tell you right now that he's a pigheaded sonofabitch who won't fudge an inch. What he says is what it is."

"It was a rear-end collision; what does he have to fudge?"

Dockett's sandpaper voice had rubbed Shapiro's already raw nerves.

"You've got at least eight defendants that I can count here. What if the van driver had only ten thousand in coverage—or no coverage at all? The driver could be just a small player in all of this. Hutchins could mess things up for us on the other deep pockets—if he doesn't understand the facts. I'll have to see him right away, try to set him straight."

Nick hesitated for a moment. "I want pictures of everything: the scene, the car seat, the car—"

"I'll have Hutchins stop traffic on the interstate for ten minutes; early Sunday morning's the best time to get good shots of the scene."

Shapiro rolled up his other sleeve to the elbow, and for the first time that morning, sat back in his chair.

"Sounds good, Jerry. Very professional."

"I'll need to take at least fifteen witness statements. Take me about a week, provided...."

Shapiro knew what he was about to say. Provided he stayed off the booze.

"When I win this one," Nick said, "there's a nice bonus in it for you."

"Wouldn't that hit the spot. In the meantime, I'm going to need a few hundred bucks to get started."

Shapiro opened his desk drawer and stared at the Irati retainer.

"Do you take cash?"

CHAPTER 9

Nick didn't make it to the office until ten o'clock the next morning. He stayed in bed until he got the details of the day worked out through dreams. It wasn't the best way of managing one's behavior, but it beat the harshness of reality, which usually had nothing to do with how things should go.

"Of all days to come in late," Carol Emry said, "the phone's been ringing off the hook from the ad."

For a moment Shapiro didn't know what she was talking about. He stood in front of her desk, staring.

"Things must be tougher out there than I thought," Nick finally said. "I guess not every hot-shot out of law school is making a hundred grand to start."

"From the sound of the calls, they're not making ten cents. I screened out the flakes, and women who sounded fat—"

"How can someone sound fat over the phone?"

"I know how you hate fat women. I've set up interviews starting at two o'clock."

"Today?"

"No, next month. Don't you want to stop paying on the ad?"

Shapiro rubbed his cheek. He'd forgotten to shave.

"Who's coming?" he said.

"A Mark Solomon, Grady Hess and a Richard Dirkin. I put them at half hour intervals."

"No faxed resumes first?"

"They don't have any resumes."

Shapiro sighed and shook his head.

"They probably don't have any brains, either. Which would be O.K., provided they were ethical, which I'm sure they're not, either."

"They sounded anxious for the positions."

"What positions? It's to rent an office. Did you tell them anything?"

"Do I have to do everything for you? You screw them yourself. I'll be there to pick up the pieces later on if need be."

Shapiro sniffed the air.

"What's that perfume? You haven't worn it before."

"Ode du Pussie, very French."

"Very funny, sorry I asked."

"Want some?"

"Carol."

"For your wife."

"You know what I want, and two sugars, please."

"Here is your other message. Jerry Dockett called."

"Maybe he's gone straight after all."

Carol didn't comment.

"Bring my coffee."

"We've got problems with the child seat, Nick."

Dockett's voice sounded sober, but out of breath, like he was concerned.

Shapiro rolled his eyes back, tucked the phone

into his neck and cracked his knuckles.

"Here it comes, I knew this case was too good to be true. Let's have it, Jerry—right between the eyes."

"Hutchins, the highway patrol investigator in charge, is in the middle of completing his homicide report. He showed me the baby seat. It's not a child car seat, it's just one of those infant carriers, you know, the kind women walk around with. It wouldn't protect an armadillo in an accident."

"Oh God."

"That's not the bad part."

"Twist the knife in deeper."

"Hutchins is going to charge your man with manslaughter in the death of his own baby—for using an improper infant car restraint that contributed to the death."

Shapiro dropped the receiver on his desk. He held his head in his hands. That old familiar pang of defeat grew like a chia pet in the pit of his stomach. He picked up the phone, slowly putting it to his ear.

"But it looks like a car seat, right?" Shapiro said.

"Does to me—and if I was fooled, what was in the mind of King Albert Alonso and his wife when they bought the damn thing?"

Shapiro's breathing became easier, deeper. His mind started to clear, like after a good run.

"Were there any warnings on the seat, you know, like 'do not use as a car seat,' something like that?"

"None. It'll be another month before the homicide report's ready. Hutchins won't give me the seat—he needs it as evidence for the district attorney against Alonso. I got some good pictures, though."

"Jerry, you've got to call in some chips on this one. Get Hutchins to back off on the criminal charges. Christ, the baby's dead, what does he want to do, torture the Alonsos? It'd ruin any chances in the case."

"Hutchins is a cop, they're all stupid. I'll see what I can do."

Shapiro heard the flipping of notebook pages.

"I've located the car," Dockett said, "at Randall's Towing, over in the north end. Man, what a mess, rear end is split open and crunched up like a slinky."

"Pictures?"

"More than a Japanese tourist at a strip show in Paris."

"I'll have it towed to my expert, David Halgers. He's got a place over in Tinytown where he does his thing."

"Not so fast, Nick. In a deal like this, everyone gets his pound of flesh. Randall's won't release the car until Hutchins says so."

"I know...and the putz needs it for evidence against King Albert."

"You got it. By the way, Randall gets twenty bucks a day for the storage."

"But the car's totaled out."

"That's the whole point with these towing people. They know the car's worthless, but they also know you need it for the case. They'll keep it until it's released, then try to shake you down for five grand or so to pay—"

"I'll steal it from them first."

"Don't get too excited, I found out the going rate's fifteen hundred, no matter how high the storage charges are. When it comes time, start off at a grand, offer cash, maybe you can get it for less. Better get your man Halgers over there right way to examine the car, before old man Randall gets a bug up his butt and dumps it for more valuable space...Nick, you there?"

"Wish I wasn't. I should've referred the case out."

"Don't think so negative. I haven't even started with the witness statements yet, and you don't have the experts' reports."

"I may not even have a client. He could go to prison because of some lunkhead cop."

"You're a lawyer, get the right answers for him."

Shapiro looked to the ceiling.

"Jerry, if I knew where to find them, I'd have been out of this business years ago."

Whenever his back was up against the wall, there was always a place Nick could seek solace: his law library. It was the greatest single piece of overhead in the office. Those lawbook people were the smartest in the world. The law kept changing; new cases and precedents decided everyday. The books had to be constantly updated, replaced. It would be the same as if every great author who had ever lived kept changing his or her work every six months or so, and everyone who had his or her book on their bedstand had to buy a new one to make sense out of the story.

The library also served as a conference room, in what used to be the kitchen of the building before Shapiro converted it to an office. He sat at the formica table that was too large for the room, thumbing through the index to the case-annotated state statutes. Under the subheading "Automobiles, Child Restraint Devices," his index finger came to rest on Section 316.529.

He went to the statute books, a fine set of volumes that filled an entire floor-to-ceiling bookcase.

Volume 20 contained the statute he was looking for. He pulled it down, and opened it on the table.

The first part of the law was straightforward, requiring every child aged five and under to be secured in an approved restraint device when riding in an automobile. The penalty for failure to do so was a ticket for the infraction, no more severe than failing to yield.

Then, at the very end of the statute, there was a subsection that Shapiro had to read over again three times before he could believe it. It said that the failure to utilize an approved infant seat could not be used as a defense in any civil action brought by the parents of a child injured or killed in a car accident.

Did God himself write this law at the base of Mt. Sinai?

Corporal Hutchins' belief that the seat was a contributing cause of baby Alonso's demise was actually the best expert testimony Shapiro could have for a claim against the manufacturer for failure to warn consumers, because the company couldn't use it as a defense.

The more Hutchins wanted to prosecute King Albert; the more the manufacturer would have to pay.

It was almost too good to be true.

CHAPTER 10

"Your two o'clock interview is here," Carol Emry said.

Nick looked up from his desk; she was standing in the doorway.

"May as well get this over with fast," he said. "There's nobody as good as me, and that's what I'm looking for—me."

Carol smiled, and turned her back slightly, half-facing her desk.

"This guy's definitely not you, Nick."

She returned to her computer screen.

Nick got up, walked to the reception room door and opened it.

"Excuse me," Nick said to a man who was sitting in reception, "there's supposed to be someone here to see me. Did anyone leave?"

"I'm here for the interview."

"You?"

Nick stood there with his hands at his sides. He examined the man, from the skullcap on his head and the beard on his face, down to the fringed tassels hanging out over the belt.

"The synagogue's down the block, mister," Nick said.

"I was there for the *minyan* this morning. It's my *shul.*"

"You're a lawyer? I mean...you look kind of old to be just starting out."

"I'm Samuel Kaplan." He held out his hand and shook Shapiro's. "My friends call me Shlomi. I passed the bar ten, fifteen years ago, but I never practiced. Had some things to straighten out first."

"Don't we all? I'm Nick Shapiro." Nick just stared at Samuel Kaplan.

"Is the position still open? It's convenient for me here; I live in the neighborhood."

"Come into my office."

Nick pointed and Kaplan led the way.

Carol rolled her eyes as Nick walked past her.

"Have a seat, Mr. Kaplan."

"Shlomi, please."

Nick sat and started turning a dagger letter opener in his hand.

"Look, are you a rabbi or something?"

"I studied under some of the best when I was in Israel, but no."

"What made you come back to the States?"

"It was time. I wanted my family, my wife and children, to live better. Life is hard in Israel. Arabs taking potshots at you with rockets and machine guns doesn't help much either."

"I didn't mean to deceive you by the ad, but all I'm offering is office space, no salary. You do a certain amount of work for me each week in exchange for the space, that's the deal.

"That's the best news I've heard in a month of pounding the pavement and knocking on doors."

Nick was about to laugh, but didn't. He set the dagger letter opener on the desk.

"How many kids you got, Shlomi?"

"Seven."

"How in Christ's name are you going to support them here?"

"In his name, I don't know, but Hashem will provide. I look at this as an internship. Interns aren't supposed to make a lot of money, right away. I need to learn from someone who knows."

Nick had forgotten how to read Hebrew the day after his bar mitzvah. But he knew the word used by Kaplan was another way of saying God's name.

"I don't know, Shlomi; we're so different, you and me. All the restrictions you've got to keep up with, dietary laws, holidays—it's not compatible with the type of in-the-pits law I practice. Especially the big case I want to get you involved in."

"We're not different. You've just drifted away a bit is all."

"Yeah, like all the way across the universe. I haven't seen the inside of a synagogue for thirty years."

Kaplan's clear blue eyes smiled. He was handsome beneath the beard.

"Then we can both learn from each other," Kaplan said.

There was an easy way about the religious man. Nick liked him, despite the strange appearance. He'd never known an Orthodox Jew before; they kept to themselves. But here was one who had the same profession as Nick, willing to start at the very bottom, just as Nick had done.

"Have any legal experience?" Nick said.

"Library research. I'm good with the books."

"You can't just bury your nose in appellate cases. Here, you have to be a cop, a prosecutor, a public defender and a shrink, all rolled up into one. Could you handle it?"

"So long as it's not on *Shabbas*." (The sabbath.) "And where do you think all of this law and procedure came from to begin with?"

"Let me guess."

"That's why we love the law."

"We?"

"Our people, you."

"Leave me your resume, Shlomi Kaplan. When I'm finished interviewing, I'll call you either way."

"No you won't. But here it is anyway."

Shlomi reached into his case and gave Nick a resume. The men stood and shook hands.

"Don't you want to know why I went to Israel to begin with?" Shlomi said.

"To find yourself, I suppose."

"To find the meaning of life."

"Did you find it?"

"Would you like to know?"

"Is it a full moon?" Carol said.

Nick, struggling through a first draft of the Alonso complaint, didn't hear her at first. He put his pen down.

Carol said, "First we get Shlomi Kaplan and now—"

"Don't tell me—it's a priest who knocked up his girlfriend, and that prompted him to go to law school and...."

"Come see for yourself. But you'd better clear this one with your wife first."

"What's she got to do with it?"

Nick went to the reception room door and opened it for the next interview. Then he made his classic *faux pas* of staring right where women with low-cut blouses want men to stare.

"Are you Mr. Shapiro?" the young woman said.

Nick's eyes drank her in. How could someone built like this be a lawyer? She was dressed like she was going out for the evening: full black gown, high heels, hair done up.

"You must be Ms. Hardonman."

She laughed. "Handeman, Rene."

"I said that, didn't I? Won't you come in?"

Carol didn't dare look up from the computer screen as they walked by. She hid the grin on her face.

Ms. Handeman sat in one of Nick's chairs.

He closed the door and took his own seat.

"How long have you been out of law school?" Nick said.

"A year. I've had two jobs already."

"Courtroom experience?"

"Some, but I didn't like any of the people I worked for, so I moved on. Thought I'd try it on my own, you know, keep the expenses down, try and make a few bucks."

"Ever try a case in court?"

"I could handle it."

Nick made a small grimace.

"You'd have to give me twenty hours a week. In exchange you get the office, phone, photocopies, library, the whole bit."

"Your ad said something about referrals."

"Divorces mainly—"

"I like family law."

She'd be a good one to hold Barbara Irati's hand.

Nick stared at her. She was too young, too pretty to make it in this business. Every lecherous judge would try to get her in the sack before she finished arguing her first motion. Forget about her opposing male counsel.

"Where did you work before?"

"I'd rather not tell you."

Nick liked the way she was honest about it. But who could concentrate with her around?

"Hope it's not something I wouldn't want to find out later on," Nick said.

Rene shook her head.

"They'd lie if I told you anyhow."

"A lawyer would lie to another lawyer?"

"Especially to another lawyer, for the pure pleasure of it."

They both laughed.

Nick reviewed the resume she handed him.

"My God," he said, "you were top of your class. Tell me, you could be working anywhere you want, Wall Street, name your price. Why here?"

"It's the only way I'm going to make it in this business, on my own. Then the only person who can take advantage of me is myself."

Nick picked up a pencil, and tapped the eraser on his desk for too long a time. He was staring again.

"I've got five more interviews," Nick said. "And frankly, I was looking for someone with trial experience to assist me on a big case that's coming up."

He wanted to jump right across the desk, hold her in his arms, caress her smooth cheeks with the back of his hand and tell her how perfect she was for the job.

She seemed to frown.

"I'll call you tomorrow," Nick said, "after the other interviews."

Nick walked her to the door. He stood too close to her, smelled her perfume, and looked at the shoulder-length black hair that flowered out to accentuate her face.

"I really want this office," she said.

Nick was weak. Is this what they meant when they said there's no fool like an old fool? He wasn't that old, was he?

"We'll see," Nick said.

Carol brought a fresh cup of coffee into her boss's office.

"That was interesting," she said. "Need a change of underwear?"

Nick sipped the hot coffee, then looked up at Carol.

"Don't press your luck," he said.

"If she's in, I'm out," Carol said.

"Believe me, I've got to take on someone else— for both our sakes."

"Don't be so sure."

"What's that supposed to mean?"

"There are no more interviews."

"We had five set up."

"They've all canceled. Must've found out how much you were paying. Should I run the ad another week, or—"

"Or do we go with the rabbi and the brilliant Barbie doll?"

"The ad'll cost you another three hundred."

"Those thieves. We're in the wrong business, Carol."

"I might not quit if you treat me right, even if you do take her."

"Don't I always treat you right?"

"If I catch you so much as sniffing her chair when she gets up, I'm history."

Nick sighed.

"At some point, my dear, we're all history. That's one thing that always repeats itself."

CHAPTER 11

Marilee Shapiro poured herself a glass of white wine. She paced back and forth across the kitchen floor, taking big sips of it.

"Why do you have to hire a woman lawyer?" she said to Nick. "There must be ten thousand guys with law degrees looking for a job in this town."

"The other one's a man," Shapiro said.

"An Orthodox Jew. That's almost as bad—in reverse—they hate women."

"It's just that they follow Genesis literally, you know, the part where God says that men will dominate woman for what Eve did."

"That's not all he did to women for what Eve did."

"Oh, so it's that time of month, I was wondering what was bugging you."

Marilee threw the wine glass at a corner of the room. It was empty when it shattered against the wall.

"Why do you always blame it on that? Can't a woman get emotional about something without being accused of PMS?" Marilee looked down at the floor. "Now there'll always be some young chippy sniffing around you, learning at the heels of the great legal guru. It'll take her ten minutes to fall in love with you, Neal."

"Would you get a grip? That's what the legal profession is these days, women. They're all over the place, judges, prosecutors, trial attorneys."

"They're all a bunch of cunts."

Marilee took another wine glass from the cupboard and refilled it from the bottle.

"You wouldn't say that if our daughter became a lawyer."

"Cunts."

"My, my, Marilee."

"You've given me cause to worry in the past, Neal."

"It was all in your paranoid little head," Shapiro said. "If you try to bring up yesterday's non-news again, it could produce the same bad effects you're trying to avoid." Marilee held up her hand in a peace sign.

"You're right, as usual, Neal." She hesitated a moment, then took a long sip of her wine. "I've got to show that mansion out in Highland Park again tonight."

"How many times have you showed that house at night in the last month? Why can't they schedule the appointments for you during the day?"

"It's the safest neighborhood in town."

"There's no place that's safe. I'll go with you."

"No...I mean there's nothing to worry about, really."

Marilee held herself in her arms and scratched both of her triceps at once.

Nick got up from the table and poured himself a scotch. He stood by the counter, swirling it around with a finger.

"It's Thursday night," he said.

Marilee gave him a confused look.

"We were supposed to have a family dinner?" Nick said. "You, me, the kids, every Thursday. That was the deal."

"Who thought you were serious about that?"

"Where are the children?"

"Debbie's at the mall with her friends. Tommy's at David's, staying over for dinner. I put something in the microwave for you. Heat it for two minutes and—"

"I wanted to have dinner with you."

"My appointment's early tonight."

Marilee filled her glass again. This time she gulped it dry.

"I've never seen you drink like that," Nick said.

"It's only wine."

"Still."

"We wouldn't be able to go out with the other one you hired," Marilee said. "What's his name—Shlomi Kaplan? Those people keep kosher."

"We could go to a kosher restaurant—who's even talking about going out with them?"

"Dressed the way they dress, I can just picture his wife: fat, no shape, her hair covered, skirt to the ground."

"You shouldn't be complaining about that, it's the way you want every other woman in the world to look for me."

"I've really got to go, Neal."

"So go. I'll eat alone, in front of the TV Me and the sick cat."

"How many nights did I have to do that when you were out...working?"

Shapiro knew that if he said one more word it would escalate into a major fight, maybe even physical. It had happened in the past. A few punches going both ways, no major damage, but a lot of guilt afterward.

The smartest lawyer was the one who knew when to shut up.

Shapiro watched from the front room window as Marilee pulled out of the driveway, onto the street—then sped off into the night.

The next morning Nick was in the office before Carol arrived to open up. It was the first time he'd beaten her there in five years. He even made the coffee.

A skeleton draft of the Alonso complaint sat on Nick's desk. There were lots of blank spaces in each of the counts for negligence and breach of warranty. There were even blank counts for defendants as yet unknown. Perhaps Jerry Dockett could fill them in. There'd have to be deep pockets somewhere. The preliminary accident report Dockett had obtained showed that both the van driver and the stalled vehicle in front of the Alonsos had only ten thousand dollar insurance policies. Hardly enough for a dead baby. Someone else would have to pay, and pay big.

When Carol opened the front door, the suction in the small office building pulled every inside door and window in an inch. It was how Nick knew someone was coming, the noise. This was sometimes a valuable tool for ducking out on a client disgruntled with life in general—and attorney Nick Shapiro in particular.

Carol's head appeared around the doorjamb of Nick's office.

"Did you spend the night here?" she said.

"I'm antsy, wanted to get the Alonso complaint finished and filed."

"And in the meantime you're not doing any dictation on the bread-and-butter stuff. You can't try the Alonso case if you can't pay the bills. Where did you sleep last night?"

"Can't you tell by the contented look on my face?"

"Thought maybe Marilee booted you out."

"Cup of coffee, please?"

"I'll make it again, fresh. You don't know how to make it."

"I thought you liked the way I make it."

"Don't tease, Nick."

"Who's teasing? That's a great outfit, new? I can't believe how long your legs look in it."

"Now I know you had a fight with Marilee last night."

Nick pointed to one of his chairs.

Carol sat.

"Let me ask you something," Nick said. "Do you think Marilee could be having an affair?"

"Her? Not a chance."

"She works a lot at night these days."

"So, have Jerry Dockett tail her."

"I'd never do that."

"Afraid to find out the truth?"

Carol paused a moment.

"Nick, a piece of advice from someone who's been there: don't go looking for problems where none exist."

"All right, doctor. You can bring me that coffee now—and whatever files you think need to be worked on."

"Too bad she didn't kick you out. I'd take care of you a lot better than she does."

It was ten-thirty. Nick had his face buried in a mortgage foreclosure file when Carol buzzed him on the intercom.

"David Halgers is on line one."

Nick crossed his fingers.

"David, hello. What've you got for me?"

"First of all, the grand you gave me to get Alonso's Ibis out of hock wasn't enough. Those greaseballs at the towing lot shook me down for another three hundred."

"Put it in your statement."

"With interest, Nick. Anyhow, I got the car back to my shop, storing it inside to preserve it from the elements. It's two hundred a month for the storage."

"Outrageous."

"Standard. And it's just the beginning. At some point we're going to need a real automotive engineer—a PhD—to go up against the Ibis big boys. I'm just a hands-on guy, good enough for now, but for trial...."

"We'll cross that bridge when we fall through it. What did you find?"

"Inferior quality metal on the chassis—too thin and brittle. Destroyed the integrity of the whole rear end. You should see how this thing caved in. The baby never had a chance."

There was no response.

"Nick? You there?"

"Keep talking."

"Was the car ever in a rear-end accident before?" Halgers asked.

Nick flipped through his notes of the initial conference with King Albert.

"Two years ago, minor fender bender, left rear."

"You're going to have to make the garage that did the repairs a defendant. I don't think their work had anything to do with this accident, but you can bet the Ibis people will point the finger at the garage, alleging faulty repairs."

Nick made notes in his yellow pad. Two more defendants, now it was up to eight.

"So you think there's a case against Ibis?" Nick said.

"Bankable. What's your time frame, Nick?"

"Hope to file the lawsuit by the end of next week."

"Then get ready to be papered to death. I've been on the other side of Ibis before. They hire the biggest and the best law firms to defend themselves, and they don't take anything lying down."

"Hey, with guys like you in my corner, it's them who'll need to watch out."

"Keep up the strong false front, Nick. You're going to need it."

By noon, Nick had finished the two new counts of the complaint against Ibis and the repair garage. He loved putting codefendants at odds with each other. Then he could just sit back and watch them fight it out.

His office door was pulled in by the suction of air.

"Jerry Dockett's here," Carol said over the intercom.

"I know."

Nick greeted Dockett at the reception window. He opened the door for the big private eye. No smell of booze.

"Didn't think I'd hear from you today," Nick said.

They were standing in front of Carol's desk.

"I found out something you really need to know," Dockett said.

Nick didn't like his tone. Had Dockett discovered something?—the torpedo Nick knew had to exist that would explode the whole case to dust, just like every other good case in the past.

Nick looked to Carol, then back up to Dockett.

"Just break it to me easy, will you, Jerry? I can't take too much pain all at once."

"Who's talking about pain? Christ, get this, the van driver was in the course and scope of his employment with an outfit called Taylor Plumbing, Inc. at the time of the accident."

Nick sort of fell back up against the wall. He wasn't able to talk.

"They've got three million in coverage," Dockett said. "I sweet-talked the boss's secretary into giving me a copy of the policy. Here."

Dockett and Carol smiled at one another for the first time in months.

"You've got a few problems with the other defendants," Dockett said, "but this one's a lock. All you've got to prove to the jury is that the driver was on his way out to a plumbing job for his employer, then you've got them by their lead pipes."

Nick thought for a moment.

"But that's when these guys fight the hardest—when they know they could lose it all."

"Pal," Dockett said, "a fight like that I'd like to be in everyday."

By three o'clock Nick had finished the entire rough draft of the Alonso complaint, in longhand on yellow sheets. He leafed through the pages once again, caressing each as if they were insurance drafts made out to him—for a million dollars each.

Carol Emry's voice came on the intercom.

"Barbara Irati's on the line, says her husband threatened to kill her. She needs a restraining order."

"Like a piece of paper's going to stop a guy from punching out his wife if he wants."

"At least the police will come out and make an arrest. Talk to her, Nick."

"Start filling out the papers for the TRO. She can come in tomorrow to sign. We'll file the petition, get a hearing date down the road—"

"She needs it now, Nick—she's really frightened. You'll have to bring her in to see the emergency judge this afternoon."

"This afternoon's over—she can wait until tomorrow, like every other client."

"Nick."

"What is it with you women? Some sisterhood kind of thing?"

"Something like that."

Nick patted the Alonso draft one more time, then pushed it over onto a corner of the desk.

Into each life a little acid rain must fall.

CHAPTER 12

There was action in the office again.

It was something Nick hadn't seen for a long time: all the offices filled with attorneys, the telephones ringing, business machines humming away. He liked the sounds.

Shlomi Kaplan and Rene Handeman sat in the chairs in front of Nick's desk, "beauty" and "beast."

Rene held in her hands what Nick thought was a final draft of the Alonso complaint.

"My reading of the Wrongful Death Statute," she said, "requires the specific damages to be alleged in each count, separate from the parents' own injuries."

"I've done that," Nick said. "It's right there in black and white."

"I took a seminar on this, Nick, three months ago. It's the state of the law. If you file the complaint in its present form, it'll be dismissed on a motion, and you'll have eight sets of attorneys taking potshots at it. I'm telling you, it won't stand muster."

How did she know? She'd never tried a case in her life. Just because she was pretty and young and up on the law didn't also mean she was smart.

"What about it, Shlomi?" Nick said.

Shlomi stroked his beard.

"I have no idea. I've never seen a complaint before. They don't teach you about lawsuits in law school—only the theory behind them."

As dumb as it sounded, that was true.

"Great," Nick said. "I could have used your office for someone who knew something."

"Have faith, Nick. Once I learn something, I really know it—know what I mean?"

"No."

Nick looked at his two charges and let out a deep breath.

"What have I gotten myself into?"

Rene dropped the seventeen-page document on the desk.

"A great case," she said. "Let me fix up the complaint a bit, then you can look at it. If you think I'm wrong, then file it your way."

And she was so logical, and nice about it, too.

"Dictate the changes on a tape and give it to Carol," Nick said. "She can plug it into what I've already got on the computer—then let's see."

Rene picked up the draft and left the room.

Shlomi's head started to follow her out, but then he checked himself.

"She's pretty, isn't she, Shlomi?"

"We're not supposed to think about these things. It's why our men sit on one side of the synagogue and the women on the other."

"You're human, aren't you?"

Shlomi nodded with turned down lips.

"That's also why our women dress with the long skirts, heads covered, no flesh showing anywhere. Remove the temptation; then it's gone."

"What did you do before you—?"

"Became Torah observant? I was a student—smoked a lot of grass, dropped acid on occasion—"

"You were a hippie?"

"An original, slept on the sidewalk in Haight-Ashbury."

Nick rubbed his chin.

"My, my."

"The last ten years have given me insight into the human condition. People behave in certain ways, they have certain jealousies—it's all in the Talmud, and it's predictable what will happen if the *mitzvot* of the Torah aren't followed, God's six hundred thirteen commandments."

"I thought there were only ten."

Shlomi laughed.

"Life would be too easy then."

"So, how do I get my twenty hours of work a week out of you, Rebbe Kaplan?"

"Books. Send me to the law library. What do you want me to research?"

It was a fundamental issue, but Jerry Dockett's discovery that the van driver was working for a company at the time of the accident needed legal precedent to support the liability of the employer.

"You know what 'Respondeat Superior' is? Give me a memorandum of law that'll lock in the plumbing company and also serve as a basis for some good jury instructions on the issue. I hate doing jury instructions."

"Jury instructions?"

"Just do the memo, Shlomi."

The lawyer stood and turned for the door.

"What are those fringes hanging down from your shirt?" Nick said.

Shlomi held the woolen tassels of his *tzitkes*.

"These are to remind me to follow all of God's commandments each day. Our people have been wearing them since the Revelation at Mt. Sinai, when God told Moses to have it so."

"Does it bring you any luck?"

"In a manner of speaking."

"Then maybe I'll wear them—with you around I'm going to need all the luck I can get."

Two hours later Rene emerged from her office and approached Carol's desk.

"Here's the tape with the changes to the Alonso complaint. Nick wanted it."

Rene rested the cassette on Carol's desk.

Carol pushed it to the side and looked up the length of Rene's legs, from her skirt hem to her eyes.

"Nick never told me about it. He also never said I was to do any of your typing."

"For my own things, I do my own typing. You've already got this on the computer."

Carol seemed to be checking out Rene's hair and sniffing the air after her perfume.

"Do you think you're dressed properly for a law office?" Carol said.

"Too nice for this office; O.K. for downtown. You don't expect me to come in jeans and a tee-shirt like I've seen you do."

"I'm not so certain I like the tone of your voice."

"I know I don't like yours."

"He's married, you know," Carol said.

"Nick? So what?"

Carol picked up the tape.

"How much is on here?"

"A few deletions, some additions on the damage clauses of each count. If you'd rather I did it over again from scratch...."

Rene reached for the tape.

"It's all right," Carol said. "I'll do it. Besides, I'd like to see your work—what you think you know, and what you actually do. There's never been another woman in this office."

"Then why don't we just try and be friends? We're going to be working together a lot on this case over the next several months."

"Just remember to keep your tits out of my boss's business, and we'll get along fine."

"Then you make sure to keep yours out of mine."

CHAPTER 13

Richard Greeson, the premier divorce attorney in Harris County, was too handsome to have stayed married. In his business you either went for the throat and looked like a bulldog, or quoted the law like a professor and looked like a young Errol Flynn. After five years of putting up with his affairs, Greeson's wife couldn't take it anymore. For ten years after that, he had made love to every beautiful client who had the privilege of feeling the smooth leather of his office couch on her behind.

It did nothing to reduce the enormous bill he would send them at the end of the case.

So why was Marilee Shapiro ringing the doorbell of his fancy townhouse in exclusive Highland Park at nine at night?

"Come in, my dear," Greeson said. "I was beginning to think you weren't coming tonight."

"I always come when I see you."

Greeson smiled, and closed the door.

He wore a tight pair of white pants and a flowered silk shortsleeved shirt. He worked out at the same gym as Nick Shapiro.

"Wine?" he said.

"Something stronger tonight, vodka. Have any of that pot left?"

"You're in a good mood tonight—or is it a bad mood?"

Marilee plopped down on the living room's wraparound sofa, in front of the large-screen TV. Her skirt rode up, over knees that were spread apart.

Greeson went for the drinks nearby.

"I actually had to show the house tonight," Marilee said. "Don't feel as guilty this time."

Greeson sat next to her and clicked glasses. They kissed.

"You never felt guilty," he said, "not even the first time. Different than most married women."

Marilee swallowed her first sip.

"Stand up," she said. "I want to feel your buns."

He stood before her, a foot from her face.

"God, you've got a great ass," Marilee said.

"I thought only men said that about women."

"Horny women say that about men."

She pulled his shirt out of his pants and rubbed her hands over his stomach, petting the sparse hair like the back of a dog's neck.

Greeson pulled the back of her head into his abdomen, felt her tongue in wet circles. Then he lifted up her chin so he could see her face.

"The part that bothers me is that Nick's a nice guy."

Marilee massaged her hand over his zipper.

"Divorce lawyers are supposed to have no conscience," Marilee said.

She worked her tongue harder.

"I think we need to slow down a bit," Greeson said.

He broke loose from Marilee's grip, then stepped to the coffee table, where he opened the lid of an oriental brass jar and took out a handrolled cigarette. He sat next to Marilee, lit the cigarette, inhaled, then put his mouth over hers and exhaled.

"My God," Marilee said after she blew out the pungent smoke, "that went all the way down to my navel."

Greeson blew smoke again, then let the cigarette go out.

"It's a two-hitter," he said. "No more, or you'll never make it home."

"Nick mustn't find out."

"Why don't you just tell him—not about me, of course, just that you're having an affair with someone. He'll respect you for it later on."

"When? At the same time you tell him you're going to take half of everything he owns and give it to me, including his law practice?"

"Nick's a nickel-and-dime guy. He's never made any money in the law business. You earned almost as much as he did last year, and with no overhead. His practice isn't worth anything. You're better off to stay married."

Marilee hiked up her skirt and rolled over on top of Greeson, straddling him.

"Just stick to the game plan, Richard. I don't have your twenty five thousand retainer, but I've got something to trade in exchange. That's the deal."

Marilee reached down and unzipped Greeson's pants.

He pushed his trousers the rest of the way below his knees, and felt her wet on him.

"Best divorce planning I've ever seen," he said. "Does Nick have any idea what he's giving up?"

Marilee crooked a finger on the crotch panel of her panties and yanked them aside.

Greeson slid into her.

"Nick and I haven't made love like this since I

can't remember. He doesn't appreciate me the way you do."

Greeson was slow to answer.

"Strictly business, my dear. I've got the best of both worlds: I fuck both the women and their husbands."

"For now just fuck me."

CHAPTER 14

Nick came through the front door of his office at 9:45 a.m. His eyes were baggy, and he'd missed a spot shaving.

"Look what the pet gila monster dragged in," Carol Emry said.

"I waited up for Marilee last night."

"Oh?"

"I need coffee. Thick and black."

Nick sat at his desk, staring at the diplomas on his wall, and ignoring the stack of dictation Carol had waiting for him.

She came in with the coffee, set it on the desk in front of him, then took a seat.

"Mind telling me what the hell's going on, Nick?"

Nick took a gulp of the coffee before he spoke.

"Marilee got in at eleven last night. I could tell she'd been drinking. O.K., so she had a drink with the couple who was interested in the house, talked terms—business! But when I reached for her in bed—"

"She gave you the best head you ever had in your life. Trying to get me turned on?"

"She withdrew, said she had to get some sleep. She's never done that before."

"Maybe she was tired. Haven't you ever done that to her when she's wanted it?"

"That's different...Marilee's practically a nymphomaniac. She never says no."

"Give her the benefit of the doubt. She's got a long day, work, kids."

"Bothered me so much, I couldn't sleep. Got up and watched a Three Stooges marathon until five in the morning."

"Should've called me, Nick. I'd help you get to sleep."

"Think I'll take your advice."

"You will?"

"About Jerry Dockett. If she's fooling around, I've got to know."

"Like you said before, maybe you're better off not knowing. You know, the happy clam syndrome?"

"A clam that doesn't get laid can't be too happy."

Carol got up.

"I've got work to do. Jerry'll be here later to pick up the Alonso complaint for service on the defendants. Talk to him then if you want."

"Rene didn't tell me the complaint was ready. Mind telling her to come in here, please?"

Nick's eyes narrowed as he glared at Rene across the desk.

"Nothing ever goes out of the office without me seeing it first, understand, Rene?" Nick said.

Rene wore a gray pantssuit. She sat on the sofa across from Nick, her legs far more apart than she would have had them if she were wearing a skirt.

"You already signed the last page," she said. "All I did was make the changes we discussed, got the complaint ready for—"

"You don't know what this case means to me, Rene. There can be no room for error here."

"Did you find any error when you went over my work?"

"Well, no, but—"

Shlomi stuck his head in the door.

"Are you having your first fight?" he said.

Rene blushed.

"Everything's fine, now," Nick said. "I guess. Did you finish the law memo yet, Shlomi?"

"Knew you'd ask."

Shlomi stepped into the office, and handed copies of the memo to Nick and Rene.

After a few minutes of reading, Rene said, "This is really good."

"With footnotes, yet," Nick said. "Last time I saw that was while reading a *Harvard Law Review* article."

Shlomi bounced on the balls of his feet.

"If I research an issue once, I become an expert on it for life. Told you I knew my way around a library."

"I've got something else for you," Nick said. "You can bet there's going to be an affirmative defense from the infant seat manufacturer alleging its misuse by King Albert and his wife. I want you to put together a motion to strike, with supporting legal authority. I'll hit them with it hard, right at the beginning, show them I know what I'm doing."

"Win the battles; win the war," Rene said.

"I'm right on it," Shlomi said. "And, Nick, don't worry—if I go over the twenty hours, I won't charge you overtime."

Shlomi laughed. He returned to the law library.

"He was praying in the library when I got in this morning," Rene said. "Had a prayer shawl on, and those leather strap things—"

"*Tifillin.*"

"He was in a trance."

Nick eyed Rene's legs for a long time before he spoke.

"Maybe I should go into the same trance." He gave his head a mind-clearing shake. "Did Carol call Jerry Dockett to pick up the complaint?"

"He should be here anytime."

"I need to talk to him. Maybe I can kill two snakes with one mongoose."

"I don't get it."

"Neither do I, Rene."

Carol's voice came on the intercom.

"Jerry Dockett's here. Should I just give him the summonses, or do you want to give him those 'special instructions'?"

"Send him in."

Dockett walked into Nick's office holding in one hand the foot-high stack of legal papers Carol had handed him.

"I serve these for a living," the investigator said, "you don't need to waste time telling me how—"

"Have a seat for a minute, will you, Jerry? It's not the summonses," Nick said.

"I do something wrong?"

"I think my wife's having an affair. I want you to put a tail on her, come back and tell me that I'm a crazy paranoiac who should be on Prozac."

"Jesus, Nick. Maybe you're better off not knowing."

"Why does everybody keep saying that?"

"If she is, maybe it'll just burn out fast, then no harm done."

"The happy clam syndrome?"

"Beats the hell out of the pain of knowing."

"She's showing a house out in Highland Park every night this week. Leaves home about seven, you can follow her out."

"Suit yourself. I'll charge it to the case, how's that?"

"I'll pay you directly, cash. Maybe I'll ask Shlomi to say a prayer for me that I'm wrong."

"Maybe you should."

"Nick's door's been closed all morning," Rene said to Carol at the secretary's desk. "What's he working on?"

"I think it's something personal."

"You'd never tell me, would you?" Rene said. "You're loyal to Nick."

Carol stopped typing and let the screensaver cartoon drawings come on.

"I've worked for him ten years. You really get to know somebody after that long."

"Almost like a wife."

"Much more than a wife."

Rene ran a finger back and forth across Carol's desk.

"I wanted to know if Nick was going out to lunch."

"I've already ordered a sandwich in for him," Carol said. "Want lunch with me? We're the only girls in the office; we should get to know each other better, don't you think?"

"If you don't mind fraternizing with management. Where to?"

"Sammy's?"

"Too busy, too salty. Someplace quiet, where we can get a drink. I need one to get through this day."

"Then Tony's Cave. I'll put the phones on service."

It was a fifteen-minute drive out on the beltline. The motif was early modern—everything had that streamlined look of the thirties. Tony's had only separate booths, real cushiony and partitioned off by burnished teak.

The host took Carol and Rene to a far corner, where the light was dim. The table was isolated from the booths of businessmen who were cutting deals—or making dates for the evening with women who weren't their wives.

"Tim is your waiter," the host said. "He'll take your drink orders."

"Then get him over here fast," Rene said.

"Maybe the waiter'll be cute," Carol said.

"All the waiters here are faggots," Rene said. "We used to come here once in a while when I worked downtown."

"Well, that guy sure wasn't gay. Did you see the way he looked at you?"

"Who notices? Men. They all want only one thing. Why don't they just hump one of those rubber dolls you can buy at a dirty-book store."

"Because they can't conquer a doll. They like to hunt, take their prey, then throw it back when they're finished with it, alive and juicy for the next time. I think it's genetic."

The waiter arrived, a blond surfer type. Too pretty to be straight.

"I'm Tim."

"We know," Rene said.

He looked down his nose at her, like the beautiful woman in front of him was some kind of unclean animal.

"Something to drink, ladies?"

"Bloody Mary," Carol said.

"Make mine a double," Rene said.

Carol watched the waiter walk away.

"Cute little ass."

"I'm sure his boyfriend tells him the same thing—but you know, maybe they've got the right idea. They don't have anything to do with women, and they seem all the more happy for it. I've often thought about writing men off completely."

"And go for women?"

"Why not? At least they'd understand—know what each other wants."

Tim arrived with the drinks, took the ladies' food orders, then left for the kitchen.

Rene held her glass up.

"To the success of the Alonso case."

"To our new friendship."

Their fingers touched, lingered together for a moment, until Tim returned with two house salads. He smiled at what he saw, then moved off to attend to other patrons' needs.

"You understand me, don't you, Rene?"

Rene took a sip of her drink.

"I wasn't certain at first, just a feeling. But now, yes, I think I know."

"We'd have to be discreet around the office, if Nick ever found out, I...."

Rene ran her tongue around the rim of her glass.

"I'd never let that happen to you, Carol."

CHAPTER 15

"This is a rare occasion," Nick said. "The whole family having dinner together at the table."

"And it's not even Thursday," Tommy Shapiro said.

"Bet you wish it was," his sister Debbie said. "Thursday's homo day. Probably can't wait."

Nick laughed, but tried not to.

"What kind of talk is that, young lady?" Marilee said. "Anymore and you're grounded for two weeks."

"Pass the potatoes, will you dear?" Nick said. "The two weeks always turn into two hours—why even bother with that kind of threat? Besides, I think the First Amendment gives her the right to say anything she damn well pleases."

"That's the way, Dad," Debbie said.

She punched her brother in the fat part of the arm, and stuck out her tongue at him.

"That's no way to teach a child values, by preaching constitutional law," Marilee said.

"I'm not a child, mother—I'm almost sixteen. Peace out, will you?"

Marilee threw her fork down on the plate with a piece of lamb chop still stuck to it.

"If I ever talked to my mother that way—"

"She'd make you scrub the toilet with a tooth-brush," Debbie said.

"And walk home five miles from school in thirty-degree-below-zero weather," Tommy added.

"That-a-boy," Nick said.

Tommy held up both his arms and tried to make a muscle, like a professional wrestler.

"It's nothing to joke about, Neal. These kids are going to grow up with no values whatsoever."

"Just like us."

"Speak for yourself."

Marilee looked several times at the wall clock above the stove.

"I've got to go," she said. "Debbie, I want you to do the dishes with your brother. When I get back, I don't want to see a single crumb, anywhere."

Debbie mumbled something under her breath that sounded like "she sounds drunk already."

Nick swallowed a bite of lamb chop.

"Showing the house out in Highland Park again tonight, dear?"

Marilee turned from the sink with a start.

"These new people are really interested—it'll be a decent commission."

"Hardly seems worth all this work. I'll go with you tonight."

"No...no, it's all right. If the clients come on time, I'll be home early."

"What if you don't come on time?"

"You mean 'them.'"

"Isn't that what I said?"

Jerry Dockett's white van had rust holes through both side panels. It let in cool air in summer; in winter, it increased his chances for carbon monoxide poisoning. He sat behind the wheel, parked on the swale under the low-hanging branches of an elm, kitty-corner from Nick's house.

The sun was getting ready to drop behind the horizon.

Dockett crushed out a beer can and flipped it over his shoulder into the back of the van.

"Blue sedan, blue sedan," he said to his windshield.

Marilee Shapiro didn't bother to stop at the sign. She turned left at the corner, down the hill.

Dockett turned the ignition key. There was only a sick grind. He slapped the wheel. "Don't crap out on me now!"

Almost from fear of the big man's fists it seemed, the van's engine turned over. Its rear wheels dug up the neighbor's lawn, throwing a big strip of sod over the hedge.

Dockett kept his distance; he knew what he was doing.

Plenty of husbands had taken the big fall because of him, some even at the unmerciful hands of divorce-attorney Richard Greeson. If there was irony there, Dockett didn't know it.

Dockett reached for another beer as he drove. He thought better of it, and threw it back in the cooler. It would be there later. And from the looks of things, the extra beer would be his only excitement of the night: Marilee Shapiro was headed east, toward Highland Park.

For the next twenty minutes Dockett followed her, east on Rosen Drive. He yawned, and automatically put on his right-turn signal as he approached Regan, the street Nick had given him.

When Marilee didn't turn, Dockett's blood pumped faster. "No shit," he said.

A mile later, Marilee took a left into the Regency townhouse complex and parked.

Dockett pulled over to the side of the road,

behind a high row of sparse cherry hedge. He snapped open the metallic briefcase on the seat next to him and took out binoculars. He watched at a distance as Marilee knocked on the door of number 613.

A man Dockett couldn't make out let her in. Dockett wrote the address in a notebook.

"They'll never learn," he said to the cool of the early night.

He pulled his van into the lot and parked opposite Richard Greeson's house. This was too easy. A curtain was open, with Marilee and Greeson in plain view. Greeson had his hands all over her.

Dockett worked fast. He took a few still photos first, while the opportunity was there. Then the video camera was fixed into place on the dashboard, focused and switched on. He plugged the hyperbolic microphone dish into the tape recorder, kicked in the booster, and listened in on his headphones.

"I love the way you kiss, Ricky," Marilee said.

"And you taste good, all over."

Dockett took that beer from the cooler, leaned back in his seat, smiled.

"I forgot what it was like to make love and be kissed at the same time," Marilee said.

Greeson was reaching inside the back of Marilee's stretch pants, a cheek in each palm.

"God, I love how tight your ass feels."

He slid one hand around to the front.

Marilee moaned. It sounded shrill, metallic over the air waves.

Dockett fidgeted in his seat. He played with his own zipper.

"Let's go in the bedroom, for God sakes," Marilee said. "The window's open."

Dockett ducked down in his front seat.

Still stuck together, Greeson led Marilee backwards into the master bedroom.

A light on the right side of the house went on behind a drawn shade.

Dockett placed the sound dish in his open passenger window, and pointed it at the bedroom.

He tuned it in, drank another beer, and then joined Marilee and Greeson.

CHAPTER 16

Three days later Nick stood up from his desk just before lunchtime to meet Jerry Dockett at the reception window.

"Better come in my office," Nick said.

Carol looked up from her computer screen as they passed by, but she didn't smile.

Dockett sat.

Nick closed the door and took his seat.

"All eight defendants have been served in Alonso," Dockett said. "In twenty days, it's going to snow paper in here."

"That's not what I want to hear."

Nick's white shirtsleeves were rolled up. With his elbows planted on his desk, he rested his face in his hands, as if bracing for the bad news.

"Look, Nick," Dockett said, "if you're worried about your wife, don't be. I stayed with her the whole night. She went to show the house just like she told you. I waited for an hour. She showed the house to a nice WASP couple, then came straight back home."

Nick's hands clasped in prayer to the ceiling.

"Thank God."

"So now you can concentrate on the Alonso case with no distractions."

Nick dug into his pocket and came up with a roll of cash. He peeled off a hundred and slid it across the table.

"Thanks, pal. Here's a little something extra, for the peace of mind."

Dockett took it.

"Go out and have a party on me," Nick said.

Dockett gave him a weak smile.

"Sure, Nick."

Nick moved over to his office sofa, which was against the wall next to the desk. He spread his arms out across the backrest, like he was flying.

"So, tell me," he said, "are you still owed any favors from this highway patrol investigator, Henning Hutchins?"

"I'm always owed a favor."

"I'd like to have a sit-down with him before eight defense lawyers get to pound him to a pulp. His expert opinion about the car seat is key. If there were no warnings on the seat itself, then his testimony that it contributed to the baby's death is worth big bucks."

"I'll fix up the meet."

Dockett stood, moved toward the door, but couldn't say goodbye. "Nick, there's something else...."

Dockett hesitated. Then: "You know the van driver, the plumber? His employer, I think I should follow up on that, could be another deep pocket waiting to be plucked."

Nick patted the big man's shoulders.

"I don't know what I'd do without you, Jerry."

"What was that all about?" Carol said. She made the pretense of straightening some files on Nick's desk after Dockett departed.

"Have you ever been diagnosed with a brain

tumor, then the doctor told you later that he mis-read the X-rays and he'd made a big mistake?"

"Sure, just last week."

Nick rolled up a piece of paper into a ball, and flicked it at her.

"Well, that's how I feel."

"Is that good or bad?"

"Better than my first Dr. Brown's cream soda."

Nick dropped a pencil on the floor on purpose. He reached under his open desk, where there was a clear view of Carol from the waist down. She was wearing a skirt.

Carol laughed.

"God, you haven't done that for a while."

"Maybe it's time I started again. You've been looking really good these past few days. Lost weight or something?"

Carol fluffed her hair.

"New perm and color."

"Different clothes, too. Sexy."

"It's taken you long enough to notice. But you always did wait too long."

Nick went to his door, and pushed in the lock on the knob until it clicked. He stood in front of Carol with his arms outstretched.

"Come here, baby."

She stood, faced him.

They embraced.

Nick kissed her, but the old passion wasn't in her—there was no movement, her lips were weak.

"What's the matter?" Nick said.

Carol didn't answer.

Nick remembered another time Carol had turned cold on him, right in the middle of one of their hot episodes.

"There's someone else, right?"

Carol looked up at him, raising her eyes slowly

at first, almost in apology.

"Who is he?" Nick said.

Carol remained silent.

Nick still had his arms around her waist. He lowered them down onto round hips that still felt good.

"Don't tell me you're making nice-nice with Dockett again?"

"I didn't want you to know."

Nick brought her in close to him.

Carol pulled back, adjusting her skirt.

"You're not mad at me, are you?" she said.

"I feel a little foolish."

Carol kissed his cheek.

"I still love you, Nick. It's just that—"

"There's someone else, and you're one of those one-man women."

"Something like that."

"The story of my life: when I like them, they don't like me."

"Am I still the best secretary you've ever had?"

Nick ran the back of his finger over her smooth cheek.

"And I'd do anything to keep it that way."

"Is Nick here?" Rene asked.

"He went to Charlie's to grab a sandwich," Carol said. "He's starting to get nervous about the Alonso case. I can tell."

"I haven't noticed it," Rene said. "Where's Shlomi?"

"At the downtown law library. He needed a federal citation we don't have."

"That means we're alone."

Rene sat on the edge of Carol's desk, her skirt riding up a bit on her leg so that a semiexposed thigh was close to Carol's face.

Carol rested her hand on it.

"Just we two," she said.

Rene stroked Carol's hair.

"Are you nervous?" Rene said.

She leaned forward and kissed Carol on the lips, softly at first, then round motions and pecks of tongue tip expertly aimed.

A thrill came over Carol, similar to the onset of her first orgasm. Her breathing was difficult; she felt flushed.

She kissed back.

A whoosh of air sucked at the windows and doors inside the office.

Carol pushed back from the desk. The casters of her chair slid her three feet across the hard plastic floor covering.

"Mailman," the voice said from behind the reception room door.

"He'll be gone in a minute," Rene said. "Then we can lock the front door."

An hour later Rene knocked on Nick's office door. She entered before he said she could come in.

"How was your sandwich?"

"Charlie's is Charlie's."

Rene closed the door so Carol couldn't see in.

"Carol said you wanted to see me?"

"Have a seat."

Nick slid the Barbara Irati divorce file across the desk to her.

"How are you on divorces?" he said.

"Caused a few."

"No doubt, but that's not what I mean. Some Iranian guy married a blond-haired, blue-eyed, all-American girl. He likes to beat her up."

"Women are asking for trouble when they marry these guys."

"In the beginning they're smooth talkers, so polite, well mannered, then, after the lady says 'I do,' they become chattel. They threaten to take the kids to some far-off God-forsaken land if their wives don't do everything they want. I'd like you to get involved."

"No thanks."

"Twenty hours a week?"

"Well, if he's beating her."

"She'll be here in an hour. I'll introduce you. After that, you do some handholding when she needs someone to talk to, woman to woman, that'd be a good touch. She's a nice lady, and she's frightened to death of this guy. You'll handle a few preliminary hearings, keep track of your time. This one's billable hourly."

"I'll read the file; maybe I can do something to assuage her fears." Rene put the file on the chair next to her. "I'd like to take you to dinner tonight, Nick."

"Me? I should think you'd have ten guys batting down your door trying to take you out on a dinner date."

"I didn't mean it like a date. It's hard to really talk around the office—the phones, the clients. We need some quiet time, a drink, to pick each other's brain about the Alonso case, about the law in general—"

"About those divorces you caused?"

"If you want."

Nick checked his watch.

"I'll have to make it an early one. My wife's showing a house later tonight. I don't like to leave the kids alone."

"I'll get you home before you turn into a pumpkin."

"Is that among your many qualities?"

"I'd never do anything to get you into trouble with your wife."

"Too bad," Nick said.

"I could change that if you want."

"I might want."

"What were you two talking about in there?" Carol asked Rene.

"About the Irati file."

"For so long?"

"It was only a few minutes."

"It seemed longer. Will I see you tonight?"

Rene put a finger across her lips and looked toward Nick's closed office door.

"The air conditioning vents are like telephone lines in this place," Rene said. "Why don't you come over at nine-thirty? We can watch a tape or something."

"So late?"

"Promised my mother I'd take her to dinner. She's lonely, poor thing."

"Should I bring some rubber toys?"

"Honey, I've got all you'll ever need."

CHAPTER 17

The broken reception room doorbell tried to ring. It sounded like a baseball bat hitting against a tree trunk.

Carol was already on her feet, heading to the window. The air suction had beaten the sound waves.

"Mailman."

"I can see that," Carol said to the postman. "Can't you ever just say 'Bob, Bob's here.'"

Bob, the mailman, always had a sweaty smell in the summer. It lingered in the reception area even after he left.

"I'll need some help with this stuff," he said. "I can barely hold it all."

Carol opened the door, and went out to see what it was all about.

"Did someone buy a new law library that I didn't know about?" she said.

"Where should I put it?" Bob said.

"Here, I'll help you...on the conference room table."

Now the inner office also smelled of Bob. Carol would have to use the bathroom spray when he left.

"I hope they give you hazardous-duty pay for

lifting this," Carol said.

The postman waddled out, his shorts frayed in the back, hanging off him like a used dishtowel.

Nick emerged from his office across the hall.

"What's that smell?" he said.

"Bob."

Nick stepped into the conference room and began to touch the thickly packed manilla envelopes. He always did that with the mail before Carol opened it, like he was divining for checks from clients.

Carol shook a finger at the table.

"From the names on the return addresses, I'd say these are the answers of the Alonso defendants, complete with interrogatories, requests for production, and probably a demand for the kitchen stove."

"So the snow storm begins," Nick said.

"Just like Christmas. But what I don't understand is why all eight defendant law firms are responding on the same day?" Nick read the names off the envelopes.

"It's the Harris County good-ol'-boy network. Forget about E-mail. They were all in bed together before the Internet. Look: Rundle, Forebest & Shane; Hutts & Rohan; Carter, Northcutt, Simms & Malone; all the heavyweights. They've already talked to each other."

Shlomi had come in and was standing in the doorway listening.

"And all very gentile," he said. "Is there a pattern here?" He adjusted the yarmulke on his head.

"You can bet your *tuchas* on it, Shlomi," Nick said, referring in Yiddish to his rear end. "They've already started jury selection: them against us. It's how the system has always worked."

"Are you sure you want someone like me sitting at the counsel table with you?" Shlomi said. "Against the sons of perfection?"

"All the more reason to have you," Nick said. "The contrast will drive them nuts."

A fourth voice joined the conversation.

"I suppose I come in handy to lure them off guard," Rene said, "put them off the scent just enough so Nick can lower the boom on their chauvinistic heads. I worked for Hutts and Rohan for a month, until one of the partners asked me to pick up his laundry on my lunch hour."

"Did you?" Nick said.

"Yeah. But not before I pounded open some ketchup packets on the white shirts and dumped them on his desk. His jaw dropped so far, I could see his epiglottis swaying back and forth."

Nick scratched the back of his head.

"I'll remember not to borrow your washing machine."

Shlomi had stepped all the way into the library and was looking at the envelopes.

"I'd get your laundry, Nick, so long as it wasn't on Shabbas."

"Let's get to work," Nick said, "or none of us will have any clothes to even worry about. Carol, I want you to sort everything by defendant, have separate pleading and discovery files for each. Rene, you do summaries of each answer and affirmative defense. Shlomi, you work with Rene on the summaries, then research the law on each one; see if you can come up with statutes, cases, some judge's opinion on the back of an envelope, anything we might use to counter the defenses."

"It'll take months," Rene said, "if not a year to complete all the investigation, the depositions and preliminary hearings, before we can even get the case to trial."

"Not if we all work together," Nick said.

Rene backed off a step.

"That raises a good point: what're you going to do, Nick?"

"Besides try the case and make myself rich and famous? Right now I'm meeting Barbara Irati at the courthouse on an emergency motion for a restraining order. Seems her husband threatened to shoot her if she didn't let him have their daughter. That's why I want the summaries, save me five hours of reading time."

Carol stood between Nick and Rene.

"Be careful, Nick. I don't trust people who make death threats."

"That's why they put in metal detectors at the courthouse," Nick said.

Shlomi stroked his beard.

"But they don't detect an evil heart," he said.

"Don't worry, Shlomi. I know an evil heart when I see one."

Shapiro exited the elevator on the 18th floor of the courthouse.

Sitting in the line of chairs in the hall next to the emergency judge's chambers was Ms. Katherine Ansel, Tom Budding's associate, the young lawyer who Nick had faced earlier in the Timmons's divorce. Nick had been forced into a settlement on that case because of Ms. Ansel's close friendship with the judge, Cindy Gievers. He could have asked the judge to excuse herself, but then she'd remember it the next time he had to face her on a different case. Better to get the client into a fair settlement than risk being hammered by a judge who was palsies with opposing counsel.

Not even an appeal could undo that kind of damage.

Ms. Ansel wore a tailored gray skirt suit, a little shorter than it should have been. She had not one hair out of place, and dark paint over puffy lips. Instead of doing her nails, this time she was talking to her client, a tan-skinned, emaciated-looking fellow, with matted gray hair. The man looked to be sniffling back tears after each word she spoke to him.

Nick knew who the guy had to be: Barbara Irati's husband.

"I didn't know anyone had put in a notice of appearance on this one," Nick said to Ms. Ansel. "I served the respondent with this motion directly."

Ms. Ansel shook Nick's hand, skin soft, grip firm and warm. Was Tom Budding also feeling that skin?

"We haven't filed it yet," Ms. Ansel said. She opened her briefcase. "Here's your copy, and our emergency motion for visitation."

"It hasn't been noticed. The judge can't hear your motion today."

"We'll see about that."

Nick read the three-paragraph motion that alleged that Mr. Saleem Irati had not seen his daughter, Andy, age six, for over five weeks. Nick didn't take his eyes off Irati as he read, especially the wooden walking cane next to what appeared to be a gout-bandaged foot.

"You'll have to notice your motion for another time, Ms. Ansel."

"If you don't mind, Mr. Shapiro, now that our niceties are over, I'd like to continue the conference with my client, in private."

The elevator bell chimed. The door opened, and out came Barbara Irati. Her face immediately turned red when she saw her husband. She walked quickly to Nick's side, as if for protection from Saleem.

"There are chairs around the corner," Nick said. "Come."

They sat.

Barbara dropped a shopping bag full of papers next to her feet.

"I'm glad I listened to you and didn't bring Andy," she said. "I was going to anyway."

Nick felt the momentary flush of anger. In his early years it would get him in trouble with clients, when they didn't follow his advice.

"We'd better get something straight between us," Nick said. "You must always do what I tell you in this case. I don't care how dumb or insignificant you think it is, or even what someone else you trust might tell you. If you violate that rule, not only will I not represent you anymore, but you're going to have a problem with the remainder of the case."

"My aunt's been telling me some things. I've got a girlfriend who's been divorced and she says—"

"Take everything you've heard and forget it. I'll get you through this ordeal, but you've got to follow that one rule. That, and pay every bill I send you by return mail."

Barbara looked at Nick. She'd been crying, and couldn't see through to Nick's joke.

"I'll do everything you say, Mr. Shapiro, promise."

Her hair was reddish blond; her accent was Southern. She was sincere. Nick liked her, and felt sorry for her, too. She'd gotten herself stuck with such a loser.

"He looks sixty," Nick said. "And very sick. Does he have something?"

"He's only thirty-eight, and yes, a mental problem. He can make himself look old when he wants sympathy."

"He should be a makeup artist. Where are you

keeping Andy?"

"With my girlfriend, at a motel. I'm buying a condo over in Norwood County, closing next week. Saleem won't be able to get my new address, will he?"

"Not if...not when the judge restricts his visitation of Andy."

"I need things from the house, clothes for me and Andy, her bike, some toys."

"We can work that out with his lawyer, so Saleem won't be there when you go. I'll need to send a police escort with you. There's a number I'll give you. The cops who do this duty know their jobs."

"It won't be necessary—"

Nick put his finger over his lips.

"Remember the rule."

"Sorry."

"I'll be able to get you temporary child support today, but it won't be enough. We'll ask for alimony...get another hearing in a couple of weeks."

"His brother told me that Saleem gave the tile shop to someone, just gave it away, now he's got no income to pay me anything. Says this whole thing's made him so sick, he can't even get out of bed in the morning. I think he's on medication." Nick studied his client.

"You still have that cash you took out of the house?" Nick said.

"About a hundred thousand, after the down payment on the condo. I've qualified for a mortgage for the rest."

"With no income?"

"Oh, I make money when I want to. Good with computers. I do a newsletter for doctors, dentists, CPAs. They send it out to their patients and clients each month to keep them informed, good P.R."

Nick looked at her with surprise.

"You get the articles out of magazines and things and you collate them, or something, into a newsletter?"

"I write the articles myself. Andy helps me. She's so smart, loves the color laser printer."

"You write articles on medicine and dentistry?"

"Who better to know than the mother of a six-year-old? They're not real technical pieces, things a layman can relate to. I'm told the newsletters are a big hit."

"Can you do one for lawyers?"

"Don't see why not. Probably be a little heavy on divorce articles though, until I get the hang of it."

Usually Nick hated the waiting time with a client before a hearing. After the business was discussed, the maketalk with most of them was like striking up a conversation with a foul-breathed biker at traffic school.

Not with Barbara, though. She was intelligent, fun to speak with.

For the next forty-five minutes they sat and talked, about everything, from computer software, of which Nick knew nothing, to who made the best cellular telephone.

Then, around the corner, the rumble of briefcases banging off doorjambs and laments in legalese could be heard. The prior hearing before the emergency judge had ended.

"Irati vs. Irati," the bailiff called down the hall. He read from his clipboard.

"They're ready for us," Nick said.

Nick and Barbara stood, picked up their belongings and headed for the emergency judge's chambers.

Ms. Ansel and Saleem had already entered.

"I'm nervous," Barbara said.

"All you have to do is listen to my questions, then give the answers. The judge will take care of the rest."

Nick heard female chatter coming from the judge's chambers. Could it be?

"Good morning, Mr. Shapiro," Judge Cindy Gievers said. "I believe you know Ms. Ansel. I'm running an hour behind schedule, shall we proceed?"

Now it was Nick who was nervous.

Were the judge and Ms. Ansel out for drinks last night? Maybe they double dated, Ansel with Godzilla, the judge with the 'Creature from the Black Lagoon.' He probably picked up the tab.

The parties and their counsel seated themselves at the long table extending out from the judge's desk.

"We have an emergency motion for visitation, Your Honor," Ms. Ansel said. "Mrs. Irati has hidden my client's daughter from him for five weeks. He's heartbroken over it, and so must be the child."

Nick resisted the urge to reach across the table.

"Your Honor, we're here only because of our motion for a restraining order and temporary child support...counsel knows damn well she's—"

"You'd better restrain yourself, Mr. Shapiro," the judge said.

"I'll try, Judge, but it's not easy. Counsel's client has threatened to kill my client and take the child to Iran. She's had to keep the girl hidden until the court could act to protect them both, set up guidelines until Mr. Irati surrenders his passport...and his two semiautomatic pistols. He tried to kidnap Andy out of school. Security found a knife in the man's sock; he was arrested."

The judge looked across the table. "Ms. Ansel?"

"None of it's true, and my client will so testify."

"Does he have the two guns?"

Ms. Ansel huddled behind a raised legal pad, her and the sunken gray face of her client.

"Yes, Your Honor."

Cindy Gievers sat straighter in her chair. It was past one and she hadn't had lunch yet.

"You should know my position on these matters, Ms. Ansel. Better safe than sorry. I'll grant the restraining order, set child support at five hundred dollars a month, and deny visitation until a fuller hearing can be had before the regular judge assigned to the case."

Ms. Ansel looked at her friend the judge as if she'd just stolen her prom date.

"But Your Honor—"

"I've ruled, Ms. Ansel. Mr. Shapiro, prepare an order for my signature."

Nick and Barbara Irati waited by the elevator until her husband and Ms. Ansel were gone.

"What does it mean?" Barbara said.

"For at least the next month, you can maintain the status quo, get yourself settled in, breath easy."

"Thank you, Mr. Shapiro. You don't know what a relief this is."

Nick looked into her face. She was trembling.

Maybe her husband was the evil heart Shlomi had talked about.

CHAPTER 18

When Marilee Shapiro awoke, Nick was already in the bathroom, shaving. Her hair was bunched up in cowlicks at two different places, and her face was puffy from too much wine the night before. She had used her lilac perfume to cover up Richard Greeson's cologne.

She yawned, contorting her face for a moment into an angry jungle animal.

"Are you up yet, dear?" Nick called from the bathroom. He opened the door wider. Lingering steam from his shower wafted out into the bedroom.

"If you call this being awake."

She sat up in bed and felt herself around her hips; she was wondering what she had done with her panties.

"Don't forget about tonight," Nick said.

"I already have. What's tonight?"

Nick stood in the doorway wearing only his pajama bottoms, razor in hand.

"Alzheimer's? My class reunion."

Marilee fell back onto the pillow and let out a sigh.

"We already went to one."

"That was ten years ago."

"Bald-headed men, fat women, greasy food, lies, bullshit, all those broads you probably screwed in law school."

Nick reached into the bathroom for a towel to wipe his face.

"My, my, aren't we in a good mood this morning. Could you use some cheering up?"

Nick dropped his pajama bottoms and plopped down on the bed beside Marilee. He put his hand under her negligee.

"No panties?"

Marilee recoiled. She hadn't had time to bathe from the night before.

"I think I'm getting my period."

"Now you're using that as an excuse." Nick laughed. "We can do other things."

He massaged her bare breasts.

"My tits are sore."

"You're in great shape."

"There, you see what a mess I am?" Marilee said. "Now let's call off this reunion thing, O.K.?"

"Marilee, please. I need to see these people. A lot of them are judges, powerful politicians—"

"Successful attorneys."

"I'll chalk that remark up to your monthly distress. Listen, honey, it's the best networking I could ever get—but I'm not going without you."

Marilee got out of bed and pulled a bathrobe tightly around her.

"Then I guess you're not going."

"Don't make me go alone, Marilee."

"I'm not making you do anything," she said, her back to Nick. She turned slowly and faced him. "All right, I'll go. But just for an hour. A drink, some chitchat with those boring people, and we're out of there."

"Two hours."

"Hour and a half."

Nick came to her and put his arms around her waist.

"There," he said, "now that we've got that settled...."

He opened her robe, felt her breasts and kissed her neck in little tongue jabs and licks.

"I don't mind if you are getting your period—it's been a long time."

He pulled her gently to the bed.

"All right," she said, "but nothing fancy; just stick it in and go."

Nick wasn't paying attention to what Marilee was saying. He was too busy trying to share the space that attorney Greeson had vacated not long before.

Nick left work early that afternoon; he liked to have the gym to himself on Fridays before the rush-hour crowd came. The workout woke him up, readied him for the night.

It was evening, the sun had already set, and the darkness made driving difficult in an area of remote Harris County unfamiliar to Nick.

"I can't believe how big these lots are," Nick said to Marilee, "must be two, three acres."

"Five," Marilee said. "When they turned these farms into subdivisions, it was the minimum that could legally be built, some are bigger."

"I'm told Jimmy's house is ten thousand square feet. The monthly electric bill is bigger than most people's mortgages."

"Your friend just wants to show off. They could've had the party at a hotel or something."

"Jimmy's house is a hotel—two tennis courts."

"We've got to make a right at the next mile-marker," Marilee said. "Then up on a hill on the left: these directions say so, anyhow."

Nick turned right. The lack of any street lights made the car's headlights the only source of illumination for the next thousand yards.

There was no moon.

"Looks like some commotion up ahead," Nick said.

They came upon a squad of older boys dressed in white tuxedo shirts, and black pants and bowties, parking cars out on the main road, then running back through a high wrought-iron gate in a stone fence.

Nick stopped one of them.

"Is this Jimmy Mcquire's house?"

"Yes, sir," the kid said, out of breath. "Valet parking's up at the door."

Nick turned into the gate and drove up the cobblestones, past finely manicured, rolling lawn, and professionally placed lights done in reds and blues that highlighted the flower beds. He drove past the tennis courts, with their "spa" that was larger than the Shapiro house, and past the gigantic swimming pool, finally reaching the front door of the three-story ranch mansion.

"He's not showing off," Marilee said. "He's trying to show he's royalty."

They entered the foyer. Nick took his picture-card name tag from a long table and pinned it on his shirtsleeve.

There were a lot of people standing around, in various stages of eating and drinking. Most of their faces were recognizable.

"All the action seems to be out on the back patio," Nick said. "There's a live band, too. God, I hope Louie Nato and Tom Respie show up. Haven't seen them since the last reunion."

Marilee looked beyond the vast living room, and

its African and pre-Colombian artifacts—all origi-
nals—to the wooden-decked backyard. It looked
like the floor plan of an entire other house, only
without the roof. The bar and food was out there.

"I want a drink," Marilee said. "A strong one."

Along the way there were some people milling
about the house. Nick stopped to say hello to the
ones he knew well back in school. For some reason, he couldn't recall many of their names.

One fellow had moved to New York after gradu-
ation, and practiced on Wall Street ever since.
Another quit law and became a novelist: legal sus-
pense thrillers. Nick had tried to read one, but
threw the book against the wall after forty pages.
The fictionalized accounts of what Nick knew to
be real just didn't ring true.

People kept wandering off in all directions at
the sight of a new face.

There was a winding lap pool in the back that
meandered through the wood decking. The water
lane was backlit, complete with flowing falls at intervals to swim under.

Beyond the decking and yard was a fifty-acre
lake stocked with bass and sunfish.

The lights from the other mansions around the
shore line served as small beacons on the wave
ripples and sandy shores.

The band of young musicians played sixties
music, despite the fact that their birthdates missed
the decade by several years. People danced and
crowded around the bar that was manned by two
bartenders.

"Not as many as I thought there would be,"
Nick said.

"I told you I wanted a drink," Marilee said.

Nick took her by the hand and headed for the
bar.

They didn't get far. A woman wearing a well-tailored dress and white high heels was standing by herself between the crowd trying to get to the bar. It was Maggie Ragosio, a circuit judge who had never married. The week before, she had been arrested for driving while impaired on the way home from lunch at a restaurant. She had been by herself on a Sunday afternoon when it happened.

"Maggie, dear," Nick said. "So nice to see you."

"Hello, Nick."

She was drinking a coke.

"You remember my wife, Marilee?"

"From law school, she used to wait for you by the student union until class was over."

Marilee stepped forward.

"I don't remember that," Marilee said.

"It's a problem I've got," the judge said. "Too observant of others, not enough for myself."

"I'm sorry to hear about your little...problem," Nick said. "Do you need any help, representation?"

"Thanks for offering, Nick. Hardly anyone else has even talked to me tonight. They all know I'll be out of office next election, so what good am I to them? Ray White is handling my defense."

"At least you've got the best. Look Maggie, if there's anything I can do...?"

"I'm fine, Nick...really."

"We're trying to get a drink," Marilee said. "Bring you something from the bar?"

The judge pretended to pay no attention to what Marilee had said.

Nick led Marilee away.

"Why did you say that to her?" Nick said.

"Were you banging her, too? Probably while you were dating me, doing us both. Who was better in the sack, Nick?"

"Have you gone paranoid? That was precisely Maggie's problem, too busy with the books to bang any of the guys."

"What about the girls?"

"Be nice."

Nick finally ordered the drinks. Once they were made, he handed one to Marilee, a double Dewer's on the rocks.

Nick sipped at his vodka.

He turned to take in the lake view and bumped into Louie Nato, one of the best bankruptcy attorneys in town. They had been best friends in school; now they traveled in different circles. Nick would speak to him on the phone once in five years, to refer a case.

Louie was short, with a black mustache that now spotted gray. He looked like a cousin of Nick's—and Nick had a difficult time separating the two in his mind after so much time had passed.

"You don't get older, Nick," Louie said. "You just get better looking."

His smile was wide, showing teeth that had stained over the years from constant pipe smoking.

"Don't flatter him," Marilee said. "It goes straight to his balls."

"Marilee, did you say that? Can I have some of what you're drinking? Say, you're still putting up with this guy?"

"We have a mutual understanding," Nick said. "Once a month we get to punch each other in the face as hard as we can, whether we need it or not. It does wonders for keeping a marriage strong."

"I'll have to try it next time I get married again— just make sure I don't marry a boxer." There was a pause. "How's business, Nick?"

"You know, a sole practitioner in general practice—"

"Yeah," Marilee interrupted, "it's like an elevator ride when the cable snaps."

Louie faked a laugh.

"Say," he said, "did you know Tom Respie's here? With all the money he's made, he's still the same old sweet guy. He's over by the big waterfall."

Nick drank some more of his drink, a gulp this time.

"Do you remember the time the three of us tried that shoplifting case for the PD's office in the clinical program before a jury? Tom was so nervous he asked them to find our client guilty."

"And they did, too," Nick said. "But he doesn't get confused anymore. Rung the bell for five million last week in a motorcycle leg amputation—highest verdict in the country for that type of products case. Come on, we'll all go say 'hi' to him."

"You go ahead," Louie said. "I'm going to knock around a bit, maybe there's some single women here who don't know how to throw a punch. Bump into you later."

Louie turned and left them.

Nick put his arm around Marilee's waist and led her in the direction of the waterfall, about thirty yards away. Before they got there, Nick stopped.

"What's Richard Greeson doing here?" Nick said. "He was two years behind us in school."

Marilee snapped her head around. "Where?" she said.

She saw Greeson standing by himself over near the band.

He was dressed all in black, except for the big, sparkling, diamond ring on his pinky finger. He held a drink in his hand, with one leg off to the side, like a movie star waiting for a limousine.

Marilee's heart restarted.

"He's probably crashed the party," Nick said, "trying to drum up a new divorce case or two. Richard loves to sue other lawyers in divorce cases."

"He does?" Marilee said.

"Oh look," Nick said, "those people finally let loose of Tom Respie. I'm going to grab him while I can."

"I'll catch up," Marilee said.

Nick ran ahead.

Marilee walked over to Greeson, slowly, looking over her shoulder along the way.

"What the hell are you doing here?" she said.

"Marilee, my dear. Alone?"

"Of course not. Neal."

"You mentioned you might be coming, so I asked Jimmy if I could too. I think he's afraid of me, like all the rest."

"You like that, don't you, to have men afraid of you?"

"They're afraid of what they've done wrong in their lives. When they go through a divorce, it all comes out. I'm just there to bring it out and rub it in their faces."

"For money."

"That...and other emoluments of the job."

"That I know."

"You look beautiful tonight, Marilee."

"You probably say that to all the women you're screwing when you're horny."

"I say it to women—it's what makes me horny."

"I'd like to lick every square inch of your body right now."

"Where's your husband?"

"Talking to Tom Respie. They'll go on forever."

"Then why don't we take a walk down by the lake? There's no moon. We won't be seen."

On most lawyers, a full beard makes them look

evil. Tom Respie's salt and pepper whiskers made him look huggable. Juries wanted to reach out and give him a chuck under the chin, pinch his cheeks and say, "You're such a cute little attorney. Of course we're going to give you all the money you've asked for."

"I'm no better than the next trial lawyer," Respie said to Nick. "I just have more money. More money means better experts, fancier exhibits, computer-generated accident reconstructions. Anybody can try a case, it's the getting it, and keeping it, that sets me apart."

"You get those big fat verdicts."

"And the more you get, the more you get. Other lawyers beat down my door to give me their cases. They make money, I make money. The more money I make; the more money I can make."

Nick jiggled the ice in his empty glass.

"But you must have started out at the bottom, when we got out of school. No unlimited source of funds to finance your cases like you have now."

"From tiny acorns, mighty oaks grow. Slip and fall cases turn into megabuck medical malpractice gems."

People walking by on both sides said hello to Tom.

Most didn't seem to recognize Nick.

Nick wanted to tell Respie everything about the Alonso case. Tell him how he bit off more than he could take to trial, and about the bigshot defense attorneys who were ready to pound him into a potato pancake. Respie could take over the case and turn it into a million dollars; Nick would end up with a hundred thousand in his pocket on the referral, more than he'd ever had at once in his life.

But that wouldn't be enough to change his life.

It wouldn't fit Nick's plan.

"I've got a few small personal-injury cases pending," Nick said. "The insurance companies don't settle so fast as they used to, and for a lot less when they do. It's getting tough to make a living these days."

"Notice the cases for trial as soon as you can," Respie said.

"But I'm not done with discovery, depositions—"

"It drives the insurance companies and their attorneys nuts when you notice the case for trial. They have to drop everything. They're so busy, they'll be happy to settle, afraid to get clobbered because they're not ready."

"What if I'm not ready?"

"Then fake it, beat them to the punch. It's time you started piling up you're own little acorns, Nick, my friend. We don't get any younger in this business."

Nick pictured an old gray squirrel working in a frenzy, gathering nuts and storing them away. Then he saw the squirrel run across the street and get hit by a car, its guts splattering all over the pavement.

Marilee stood up from the shore, wiped the sand off her knees and the excess semen from the corners of her mouth.

"How was that?" she said to Greeson, who was still laying on the beach with his pants down.

"Once I get the rocks out of my ass, I might be able to tell you."

"How romantic."

"Aren't you afraid your husband will see us?"

"Isn't that what you want?"

Greeson pulled up his pants and stood. He

kissed Marilee on the cheek, careful not to come in contact with her mouth.

"That would be a called a conflict of interest."

"You'd represent me anyhow, wouldn't you?"

"Certainly, my dear. It would make the torture all the sweeter."

CHAPTER 19

The law library in Nick Shapiro's office was set up like a war room, similar to that of the fictitious country in *The Mouse That Roared*. It was small but functioned with a purpose. Mounted diagrams and blowup color photos depicted the Alonso's smashed car, with its back seat where the front seat should be, and the warningless child seat. The trial exhibits lined the walls and were strewn about the floor. The long table was flooded with files, pleadings and photocopies of case law and statutes.

Rene Handeman and Shlomi Kaplan sat across from Nick, his two unlikely lieutenants, while he lectured from an enlargement of an aerial view of the accident scene with a telescoping pointer.

"It was too early to notice the case for trial," Rene said. "Right, Shlomi?"

Shlomi always tried hard not to look directly at Rene. The women in his community didn't show as much flesh as she did unless they were in a *mikva*, a ritual bath where no men were allowed.

Shlomi nodded his head slowly.

"She's right, Nick."

Rene reached across the table and grabbed the pointer from Nick's hands.

"Are you nuts, Nick?"

Nick ripped the pointer back, folded it in and fixed it in his shirt pocket, like an ink pen.

"It's the only way to move the case forward," Nick said.

"We haven't even propounded interrogatories to the defendants," Rene said. "All eight of them. Not one item of production has been received. You don't even have an expert witness for testimony about the car seat. Nick, have you got your malpractice insurance paid up?"

"I'm not looking back," Nick said. "Tom Respie says—"

"Tom Respie?" Shlomi said. "You're not thinking about turning the case over to him, are you?"

"It crossed my mind, but this is my...our case. Tom suggested an early trial notice as a way to really shake up the opposition."

"It'll turn us up-side-down, too," Rene said.

Nick hit the intercom button.

"Carol, come in here with your book, please."

His secretary entered the conference room, steno pad and pen in hand.

"What's the rush that you can't dictate it on a tape?" Carol asked.

"Who signs your paychecks?" Nick said. "Sit. Do a notice for trial in the Alonso case, jury, three weeks."

Shlomi thumbed through the legal section of the *Preview*, and stopped when he found what he wanted.

"Judge Porter's jury cases noticed now are being set in two months," he said.

"They have that in the *Preview*?" Nick said. "I've subscribed to it for twenty five years...never knew that."

"You're slipping, Nick," Carol said. "How do you

think I've known when to get you ready for trial all this time?"

"Guess there's some things even I don't know," Nick said. "That gives us two months to get ready."

"Not possible," Rene said.

"We'll have to work nights and weekends, get Jerry Dockett involved on a daily basis, witness statements instead of formal depositions, find out who the defense witnesses are, make Jerry lean on them for information—kind of like doing federal criminal defense work."

"I hate criminal law," Rene said. "You have to deal with too many criminals."

"What else?" Shlomi said.

"Let's get down to business," Nick said. "Shlomi, I want you to continue with the legal research. Over the years I've found that one of the best ways to avoid surprises at trial is to work on the jury instructions early. That way, it's almost like researching the law of the case from back to front—20-20 hindsight—only in advance."

"They never taught us that in law school," Shlomi said.

"They don't know about things like that in school." Nick turned his head. "Rene, I want you to go through the entire file, make sure we've answered all discovery requests, set for hearing any pending motions, start on the trial notebook and our order of proof. I'm putting you in charge of all witness trial subpoenas. Talk to the witnesses, go over the types of questions I'll be asking."

Rene pushed her chair out from the table and crossed two long legs.

"So what are you going to do?"

"Go to the gym. Need to trim off the stress, better than having a big lunch and getting bloated down. It'll give me the stamina to work later into the night without getting tired."

"That's important," Rene said.

Carol tried to catch Rene's eye, but Rene wouldn't respond.

Nick rolled up his left shirtsleeve to the elbow.

"I'm meeting with Jerry Dockett and our automotive forensic expert, David Halgers, at his shop at two," he said. "We'll go over the metal failures, help me solidify what his testimony's going to be. Dockett needs to get better pictures."

The telephone rang.

"Take it here on the speaker phone," Nick said to Carol.

She pressed the button.

"Mr. Shapiro's office."

"Carol, hello, this is Barbara Irati—you sound like you're in a tunnel or something—is Mr. Shapiro available?"

Nick made two slicing motions across his throat with an index finger.

Carol mouthed the word "please" to him.

"He's right here, Barbara, just a moment."

"What can I help you with, Barbara?" Nick said from across the room, in the direction of the speaker that was next to the coffee maker.

"I need some things from the house—clothes for me and Andy, her toys, a microwave oven—"

Nick pointed down.

Carol pressed the mute button.

"I can't be bothered in a fight over ashtrays now," Nick said.

"The woman needs help," Carol said. "A Tom Respie could lift the Alonso case from you this afternoon—a cash advance to the client, you know how it works—but the Barbara Iratis will always be there."

"Yes, mother."

Nick motioned upward with his thumb.

Carol released the hold button.

"Whatever you do," Nick said to the speaker phone, "you can't go to the house alone when he's there. I'll make the arrangements with his lawyer. But what if your husband has changed the locks?"

"His brother, Emir, lives right down the block. He said they'd meet me there."

"What about police protection?"

"There's someone who can go with me, a man. He knows karate."

"All right, but be careful. There's something about your husband I don't trust."

"I know—everything. Saturday morning at ten?"

"I'll ask his lawyer, Kathy Ansel, to set it up."

"Thanks."

Carol hung up the speaker phone.

"Divorces," Nick said.

"Without them, where would you be?" Carol said.

"Probably running a real estate practice, with a lot fewer wrinkles in my face." Nick looked across the table. "Rene?"

"O.K., O.K., I'll call Kathy Ansel. The bitch. Have a nice workout, boss."

"I'll see all of you back here at five for a progress report."

"I have to go to the synagogue then for evening prayers," Shlomi said. "But I can come back later."

"Make sure you say a prayer for us," Nick said.

"How do you think you've gotten this far?" Shlomi said.

Marilee Shapiro set her coffee cup on the kitchen table and answered the phone.

"Is this Mrs. Shapiro?"

The voice was deep, husky.

"Who is this?"

"My name is Jerry Dockett. You don't know me, but I know you."

"I didn't know they sold stuff over the phone during the day...thought the pests came out only at night, when it was cooler—"

"Be nasty if you want, Mrs. Shapiro, but there's someone I know, and his name is Richard Greeson."

There was a pause.

"What's this all about?"

"I think you better meet me, Mrs. Shapiro, say thirty minutes behind the Sears store at Plaza Mall, an old white van in the parking lot."

"Are you on drugs?"

"Don't make me do something I don't want to do, Mrs. Shapiro. It could be detrimental to us both."

"How do I know you're not some maniac looking to kidnap me...or worse?"

"You won't have to get out of your car, just pull up next to the driver's side of the van, roll down your window an inch, keep the door locked if you like."

"What if I tell you to go fuck yourself?"

"Then you'd ruin a lot of plans, Mrs. Shapiro, including your own."

She thought for a few seconds.

"Two minutes, that's it, then I'm out of there— and I'm bringing a gun."

"Bring a Sherman tank if you want; it doesn't bother me."

Dockett's van was parked in the near-empty lot. Marilee circled the perimeter of the shopping plaza three times before deciding to do it. She covered a kitchen knife on the seat next to her with her purse, then pulled in next to Dockett's truck.

Dockett rolled down the window, exposing his face.

Marilee cracked her window just enough to be heard over the darkly tinted glass.

"You look familiar," she said.

"Done some work for your husband, you may have seen me around."

"Wonderful. O.K., so I'm here, and my clock is running."

"There's something I'd like to show you."

Dockett lifted the TV monitor to the window, pushed some buttons on the portable VCR. The scene at Greeson's townhouse played in full color and stereo sound.

Marilee watched for a moment, then hung her head and covered her face with her hands.

Dockett turned off the VCR.

"You know," he said, "for a woman your age, you've got a great body. I've got more on audio tape from the bedroom if you'd like to hear."

Marilee finally looked up.

"Are you some kind of sex pervert? You're not getting me in the sack, if that's what you think."

Dockett laughed.

"Great oral technique, Mrs. Shapiro, reminds me of when I was in the Orient."

Marilee reached under her purse and slid the knife over to her seat, under her thigh.

"If it's blackmail," she said, "you're a bit late. I already plan to divorce my husband."

"Oh, I gathered that. I happen to know what Greeson does for a living."

"If you're smart enough to know that, then what's this all about?"

Dockett glued his fist on the open door, and

rested his chin in the huge hollow of his hand.

"What's it ever about, Mrs. Shapiro?"

"I don't have any money."

"But you will. The Alonso case. That's your plan—isn't it—to dump Nick after he wins a few million big ones?"

"Women divorce their husbands all the time."

"You'll get at least half of it in the settlement, and I want some of it. That's what this is all about."

Marilee pressed an electronic button and rolled her window down all the way.

"You don't hear very well, do you, mister? I'm divorcing my husband. I won't have any money until that happens. You can't blackmail me after the fact."

"You need to do a little more talking to that lawyer pal of yours, Greeson. If Nick sees the video now, he could file for divorce against you first, delay the Alonso case until after the divorce is final. After he wins the money, and Nick's divorce lawyer shows the videotape to the judge, you'd get nothing. It's called marital misconduct...ask Greeson."

Marilee looked around the parking lot to see if anyone was near. She could slip the knife into her purse without Dockett noticing, ask to sit in the van with him to view the tape again, and maybe come on to him. It'd be easy to jam the knife into his neck, kind of like boning a chicken.

"I don't think you've thought this through," Marilee said. "All you could get from me now is a promise, even if I wanted to go along with you, and it wouldn't be enforceable in any court."

"A promise is good enough for me. I know how to enforce it."

Marilee's heart jumped. Her mouth became dry. She licked her lips, but they didn't rewet.

"I'd like to see the video again," she said, "just

to make certain it's not doctored. May I come over there?"

Dockett started his engine.

"Maybe some other time. You can promise or not promise, Mrs. Shapiro. Either way, you know the score. My end is half of what you get."

"I'll think about it."

"There's nothing to think about."

Dockett put the van in gear and drove off.

Marilee took the knife from under her purse and stabbed it through the leather car seat. It went in easier than she thought.

CHAPTER 20

The rows of warehouses all looked the same: body shops, boat repairs, car upholstery, there were even dirty little restaurants in former oil-change bays, now in business to feed all the people. After driving in circles trying to find it, Nick made a turn out of dumb luck and saw a store front that stood out because of its neatness. "David Halgers, Forensic Automotive Engineer," the sign read. Nick parked, and walked in the front door with his briefcase in hand.

It was two thousand square feet of shiny, gray-painted floor containing wrecked cars mounted on casters, so they could be maneuvered into any position for viewing. A forklift was in a corner, for use in taking down additional cars that were stored high up in metal racks.

A big collie dog came running out from between two cars and stuck its nose directly in Nick's crotch.

"Easy, boy," Nick said. "I was invited."

Halgers, Dockett and a uniformed highway patrolman emerged from a partitioned-off office at the far end of the room.

"She's a girl, Nick," Halgers said from across the floor.

Nick backed away from the dog slowly. "The ladies used to like me," he said, "but they never showed it this much."

"Here, Rickie," Halgers said, "it's all right, girl."

The dog let Nick pass.

The men met in the middle of the room.

"This is Corporal Henning Hutchins," Dockett said. "I owe him lunch. Thought it would be a good idea for him to show us what he found at the accident scene out on I-51 before we go."

"Your homicide report," Nick said, "shows you wanted to charge Mr. Alonso with manslaughter in the death of his own child. I take it you weren't happy with the car seat the Alonsos used for the baby?"

The trooper still wore his Smokey Bear hat.

"They didn't use a car seat," he said. "It was an infant carrier." His accent wasn't from around Harris County.

"That's the whole point of my suit against the manufacturer," Nick said. "They didn't warn consumers that it wasn't a proper car seat."

Three lines of wrinkles formed on the trooper's forehead. "I don't get it."

"It looks like a car seat," Nick said. "Right?"

Corporal Hutchins nodded his head.

"It had no warnings on it anywhere not to use it as a car seat?"

The trooper nodded again.

"I gather from your report you feel the baby would not have been killed if it had been in an approved seat."

"ME's report shows trauma to the head as the cause of death—if the baby would have been contained in an approved seat, it wouldn't have been thrown around the inside of the car at impact."

Nick looked at Dockett, then back at the trooper.

"It's a fairly common occurrence, isn't it, that parents mistakenly use these infant carriers thinking they're approved car seats?"

"Our statistics show it happens several thousand times a year, resulting in over fifty infant deaths nationwide."

Dockett held out his big hands.

"Your honor," he said. "Mr. Shapiro rests his case."

"Well," Hutchins said after a while, "I see what you mean."

A fabric-snapping noise was heard off to the side, like someone was spreading sheets for a mattress. David Halgers was removing the blue dust cover from the Alonso vehicle.

"My God," Nick said. "I've never seen a car so smashed up like that."

Hutchins and Halgers laughed to each other, the kind of laugh people make when something isn't funny.

"We stare these kinds of mangled wrecks in the face every day," Halgers said. "Hard to believe the parents survived it."

Halgers, with one hand, swung the mass of steel around and out to the center of the floor on its caster wheels. The trunk and back seat of the car were gone, crushed up against the back of the front seats.

Hutchins walked around to the passenger side and pointed inside the window, which had no glass.

"The mother was in the back with the infant. The crash threw her into the front seat. Not wearing a seatbelt actually saved her life."

Nick looked in through the open back of the car. There were little drops of blood on the seat cushion that had come from the baby. When a jury saw this, it would sway them. But what would the Alonsos feel when they saw their dead baby's dried blood being thrown at them on direct examination?

"Show Nick the defective metal," Dockett said.

With a slight arm pull, Halgers turned the right, rear quarter panel around. He demonstrated with the point of a pencil.

"Look here," he said. "See how thin this sheet is? By industry standards, it's supposed to be a quarter-inch wider. And according to the manufacturer's own manual, it's five welds short. It all contributes to the destruction of the car's structural integrity."

Corporal Hutchins examined the part closely.

"Can any car," he said, "good metal or not, stand up to a sixty-mile-an-hour blow from a heavy van?"

"It shouldn't have crushed in this badly," Halgers said. "Not all the way to the front seat."

"That question is what gives juries a purpose," Nick said.

Halgers swung the car around some more, this time exposing the left quarter panel. "The only thing that bothers me," he said, "is the prior repairs here," he pointed, "from a fender bender the car had two years ago. The manufacturer is going to scream like a bride on her wedding night—they'll finger the repair shop for the structural weakness."

"The repair shop is joined in the suit as a defendant, too," Nick said. "I can play both of them against each other. Either way, we come out a winner."

Henning Hutchins stood straight, hands on his hips, just like in the DUI commercials. "Something bothers me, though," he said, "something you seem to be overlooking, Mr. Shapiro. I believe that baby's dead because your clients didn't have him in a federally approved child restraint seat. You're putting a lot of blame all over, but the real fault lies with the baby's parents."

"That's why the car seat manufacturer is a defendant," Nick said. "The parents had no way of knowing the seat wasn't approved."

Hutchins scratched the back of his head, under the brim of his hat. "I don't know."

Dockett stepped forward.

"No Harris County jury in this day and age is going to blame the Alonsos for this one—I'll go to the bank on it."

Nick checked his watch.

"Well, thanks men," he said. "It's been enlightening. I've got to get back to the office and check on progress. Things are happening fast."

Nick shook hands with Hutchins and Halgers.

"There's something I need to talk to you about outside, Nick," Dockett said.

"And I need to talk to you."

Nick and Dockett exited the shop, and stood on the curb next to the investigator's van.

"Nick, I—"

"I know, Jerry. The facts of this case look too good to be true, but there it is. Now, if I only don't screw things up. I'm going to need you to work overtime. Instead of me taking depositions, I want you to take witness statements of everyone listed on the homicide report—from the guy who swept up the street after the collision, to the toxicologist who analyzed the van driver's blood for ethanol."

Dockett wrote in his notebook.

"We don't have the time or the money to do it the right way."

"Forcing it down their throats."

"It's the only way for the small fish to eat the big ones."

"Nick...about your wife. Do you want me to still keep a tail on her?"

"I'm satisfied with what you found."

"You never know what a woman can be doing, Nick."

"Women, maybe. But I'd trust my wife with my life."

"It's not good to trust anyone too much, Nick."

"Where's Shlomi?" Nick said.

Rene leaned back in her chair, and propped a knee up against the conference table, exposing six inches of thigh.

"He's still at the synagogue, praying for God knows what. Why do you have him working on the case, anyway? What's the jury going to think when they see someone like him at counsel table?"

"What would they think if we had a priest sit at our table?"

"That you were patronizing them."

"That's exactly why the jury won't feel that way with Shlomi."

"Where the hell did you read that tactic?"

"I dreamed it, before Shlomi even showed up for the interview."

"What did your dream tell you about the outcome of the case?"

"Are you one of those people who read the last paragraph of a mystery novel first?"

Rene let her skirt creep up even more.

"I'm the type of woman who likes to know where she stands."

Nick took the seat across the table from her, and stared up the length of her neck to her eyes.

"Tell me what you've come up with while I was gone."

"You mean, while you were working out at the gym?"

"That, and seeing firsthand the results of the worst car wreck of my life. It's not something you want to look at just before trying to go to sleep."

"I'll tell you what, Nick. You handle that end of the case—I'll work on the pleadings. I'm better at paper than at blood."

"Why don't I believe you?" Nick paused a moment. "Tell me what you've got."

"Four of the defendants stonewalled our discovery requests in every way. They've objected to each question, or made some weasel explanation. They don't know what 'test' means, or 'incident,' or even 'this case'—so they've objected."

"The big firms downtown are famous for it. They don't answer anything until the judge forces them, and even then they still play games—right up until a jail commitment order is entered against them."

"Do we have time for all that?"

"No. But its O.K."

Rene sat straighter in her chair.

"O.K.?"

"We'll do an end run, get whatever information we need about the car seat and the chassis metal on our own, from the government through the Freedom of Information Act. You can get the addresses, which are in Washington, D.C., from Carol."

Rene wrote in her yellow pad.

"Carol went to the Chinese place to bring something back," Rene said. "She just left, probably won't be back for half an hour."

"Hope she gets me Mandarin beef," Nick said, "extra spicy."

Rene stood, walked a few steps, then sat on the corner of the table directly in front of Nick, legs straddling the edge. Her voice seemed to change when she spoke; it became deeper, smoother.

"You know, Nick, I went over the complaint again. The only element of damage I see is the parents' mental pain and anguish over the child's death."

"Very observant."

"In most cases the big money comes from recouping medical expenses, lost wages, future losses, and long-term care, it all adds up to millions. How much is a dead black baby worth?"

"Depends who's on the jury."

"I think you've been concentrating too hard on liability—all the expert witnesses as to cause—you've overlooked damages completely, no psychiatrists."

Nick hesitated a moment, then slammed down a fist.

"I knew this case was too big for me. How could I have missed it?"

"Relax. You didn't, yet. This is still pretrial, remember? All we have to do is get the Alonsos to a shrink. He'll diagnose them each as being severely depressed, he'll testify at trial, and we're back in business."

Rene edged closer to Nick, so that her open knees were only inches from his face.

"I knew there was a reason I hired you," Nick said.

"Because no one else applied for the job?"

"It was just a feeling—that you were another cog in the perfect wheel that this case has become. If I forget something, you'd fill in the gap before it was too late."

"I was kind of counting on you to fill in the gap for me—to help continue my legal education on a more practical basis, with you as my mentor."

Nick was staring at her now, past her thigh-high nylons, to a dark mound of semihidden, white cotton, panty. He felt the old surge rush through his body; the one he had fought so hard to control throughout the years.

"Rene...you know how important this case is to me. I can't let anything get in the way."

She put her hand on Nick's.

"I'd never get in your way, Nick."

Before he could stop himself, Nick's hands were around Rene's hips, fingers sinking into her soft leather skirt, pulling her along the side of the table, into him. Their heads tilted in toward each other. Nick's heart pounded. What the hell was he doing?

The noise of air suction against all of the office windows pulled them apart.

"Someone's here," Nick said.

Carol came into the conference room holding a brimming brown paper bag in front of her face. She set the food down on the table like a blind person who knows how to feel his way over familiar territory.

"You're here just in time for the party, Nick. I got you Szechwan chicken."

"Mandarin beef, spicy?"

Rene didn't try to hide it when she straightened her skirt in front of Carol. She combed her hair back with open fingers.

Carol looked at Rene, then back to her boss.

"Was I disturbing some important strategy planning?" She knew Nick too well—or was it Rene that she knew?

"You're just in time," Nick said. "I'm starving. Let's eat."

For the moment, the three of them ate. It was past seven, and they were hungry. Carol spread dinner on the conference table, amid the lawbooks and legal briefs. Rene passed out the paper plates and plastic utensils. Wonton soup, crisp noodles in paper packages, spicy chicken, shrimp, rice, all in cardboard containers—the kind you take gold-fish home in from the pet store—all made the rounds to each person. The only discussion concerned food, who liked what and who wanted more, and who knew of a better or worse Chinese restaurant.

The air whooshed again.

"Shlomi's here," Carol said, before anyone could see him.

Rene scooped a fat, round shrimp saturated in red sauce from a box onto her plate.

Shlomi stood in the doorway of the conference room. His salt-and pepper beard was neatly trimmed, extra rounded under the chin, making him look almost cute in a homely sort of way. He took in a deep breath through his nostrils.

"They forced Jews to eat that kind of food during the Spanish Inquisition," Shlomi said. "Those who ate it were spared, those who didn't were tortured and killed."

Nick stabbed his plastic fork into one of the boxes. "Have a shrimp, Shlomi."

Shlomi came in the room and took a seat at the far end of the table.

"If I ate that, I'd be spiritually sick for a month, probably have nightmares about Torquemada."

"He was actually Jewish," Nick said, his mouth full. "He chose to convert rather than be flayed open on a spit. I would've converted too."

"Nick," Shlomi said, "I predict you'll be keeping kosher within the year."

Carol almost choked on her dim sum.

"That's a laugh," she said.

"Laugh when I'm proven wrong," Shlomi said.

Nick pushed his empty plate to the side, and

washed down the remnants of dinner with a last gulp of Coke from the can.

"All right," Nick said, "enough of Kriswell Predicts—let's get down to business. What do you have to report, Shlomi?"

Shlomi pushed some papers around in a file until he found what he wanted.

"I'm not so certain that the statute we found prevents the Alonso's failure to use an approved car seat from being admitted in evidence against us."

"The law's clear on that," Nick said.

"There are several precedents that hold differently, in a death case."

Nick envisioned a tumbling house of cards, after he'd just placed the last one at the top of the castle.

"You'll have to go to the law library at the courthouse," Nick said. "Get out-of-state authority that's on our side. Anything that'll keep blame against the Alonsos out of evidence."

Shlomi wrote in his file.

"Carol?" Nick said. "What've you got?"

She looked up from the last of her dinner, and wiped the corner of her mouth with a napkin.

"Has everybody digested their food? In the mail today was the defendant's joint motion to take depositions from the Alonsos."

Nick swallowed hard. "When?"

"Two weeks, downtown."

"The bastards are trying to beat us at our own game," Nick said. His breathing became heavy and he kept looking around the room at no one in particular. "Carol," he finally said, "I want you to get the Alonsos in here no later than Thursday, I've got to prepare them for their depos—it'll take days. Arrange an appointment for them with that psychiatrist, the one we used on the Carter case, what's his name, Feldman, then I want—"

"Nick, will you slow down?" Shlomi said. "You're like a wind-up toy with a broken spring. Here, try this, it'll help calm you."

Shlomi pushed a thin paperback book across the table.

"A book on Jewish meditation?"

"It'll put things in a better perspective for you."

"I'm afraid the only thing that'll do that is a crystal ball."

"This book is better than a crystal ball."

CHAPTER 21

It was 11:00 p.m. Nick unlocked the front door of his house and walked in. His daughter, Debbie, was asleep on the living room couch, still in her street clothes, a geometry book open across her stomach. He tried to close the door quietly, but she awoke anyway.

"Daddy?"

"What're you doing out here, honey? Where's Mom?"

"That's why I'm out here." She yawned and stretched. "Mom made me babysit for Tommy— said I had to stay awake until you got home."

Until he got home? Where the hell was Marilee?

Nick took Debbie by the hand and helped her to her feet.

"I guess Mom's busy again. Come on, Deb. Time for bed. I'll babysit both you and Tommy."

"Like I need a babysitter."

Nick checked Debbie's profile as she rose to start down the hall to her room. She looked just like his mother, same high cheekbones, straight, regal nose. Luckily, Debbie had Nick's personality, self-confident, able to take care of herself— even at this age. Nick's mother had been lost and alone ever since his father died; it had been her own choice to isolate herself like that.

With her poise, Debbie would never have to worry about being alone.

"Goodnight, sweetie," Nick said. "I'll let you sleep another ten minutes in the morning, beauty rest."

"Can I have a car instead?"

Nick pointed a stern finger at her bedroom door.

"To bed, young lady."

She kissed his cheek.

"Goodnight, Daddy." She hesitated. "Is everything all right between you and Mom?"

Nick gave her the same look he'd give a jury in final argument, when he didn't believe in his case but played the advocate anyway.

"Everything's fine, Debbie."

Debbie smiled, kissed his cheek much harder this time, then closed the door behind her.

Nick went back to the living room, picked up his suitcoat from the sofa, hooked it on his index finger and threw it over his shoulder. He went for the bar to pour himself a strong scotch to take into the bedroom, and maybe watch some TV until Marilee got home—or until he passed out from the combination of exhaustion and booze.

He reached across the bar for a three-quarter full bottle of Dewer's.

The book on Jewish meditation Shlomi had given him earlier at the office fell out of the vest pocket of his coat, onto the bar. Nick looked at it, the paperback cover depicting a hazy scene of a far-off horizon at night, broken in the middle by a wide chasm. A tree was on one side of the chasm, a figure of a man on the other, looking across at the tree.

Nick put down the bottle of scotch and picked up the book. He tossed his coat back onto the sofa and walked to his study. He closed the door, turned the stereo to a soft jazz station, sunk deep into the overstuffed leather couch that fifty years before adorned his uncle's law office—it still harbored a faint hint of imbued cigar smoke—and began to read.

The thoughts conveyed in the book were logical—somehow Nick felt he had read it all before, in another lifetime perhaps.

Forty pages and twenty minutes later, he tried one of the "drills," which was aimed at inducing a trance-like state, so the mind could concentrate unfettered on a thought, a problem, or a relationship. The idea was to be able to thoroughly examine what one was contemplating, so that it could be seen in four dimensions, the equivalent of the German concept of *verstahen*.

A mantra was suggested by the book—different than the Eastern method, however, where any nonsensical hum could be used. In Jewish meditation a Hebrew phrase praising God, or a few words lifted from the Torah, were repeated over and over so that total devotion to the meaning of the words could induce the higher level of understanding—even the words themselves, their shapes and letters, could become the object of the contemplation.

Nick began to repeat the phonetically spelled Hebrew words, *Ribbono shel Olam*, "master of the universe," out loud, just below the level of the stereo music, at a stage whisper.

At first there was no effect. But then, after fifteen minutes of uninterrupted repetition, images of the Milky Way began to swirl around the shape of the Hebrew letters. Galaxies beyond our own, and countless billions of bright, shining stars flew past the sides of Nick's mind—who created them?

What was their purpose?

Nick kept repeating the phrase. The answer came to him, as clearly as the twinkling of the stars: only God could have created the universe, and he did it with such vastness and beauty so man would know that only God could do such a thing, and that therefore God must exist.

Nick's mind raced on. He had just had his first original religious thought. *Ribbono shel Olam. Ribbono shel Olam.*

Nick had come to the end of the universe, or more correctly, it came to him. A steep bank of high granite steps lay before him. He ascended the steps, walked past carved marble columns, into what seemed an open concrete courtyard. On the other side of it was a bench, not unlike that in a courtroom, where the presiding judge sits, elevated from the mundane position of the witness stand and clerk.

A red velvet curtain flowed behind the bench with golden Hebrew letters across its top that spelled Hashem, the word for God's name.

Ribbono shel Olam. Ribbono shel Olam.

Nick's vision became fixed on the golden letters, which then were outlined with blue, the color Nick had seen on prayer shawls in the synagogue in his youth. He had come to the divine court of heaven, where law was originated and the concept of justice born. The answer to life was just beyond the red curtain, but anyone who saw it would be struck instantly mad.

Nick tried to open his eyes, but couldn't. He'd read in the beginning of the book that this level of meditation should not be attempted without a "guide," one well versed in religious meditation, standing nearby to bring the meditator out of the trance.

Nick was drawn to the curtain. He could feel himself tremble.

"Nick...Nick?"

It was Marilee. She was tugging at his shoulder.

A force pulled Nick back from the curtain before he reached out to touch it. His eyes opened.

"Marilee—where was I?"

"Are you drunk?"

"I don't know."

"I think you are." She checked the bottle of scotch on the bar. "I should get drunk, too. The real estate contract fell through again. I'm going to bed."

"You won't believe what just happened to me."

"I'm taking a shower."

"You ought to read this book. It's stronger than any drug I've ever taken."

"You've just taken the wrong drugs, that's all."

CHAPTER 22

King Albert Alonso and his wife Muriel sat at the conference table in Nick's office. There was a confused look was on their faces, similar to fresh army recruits. Nick had just given them an overview of what they could expect at the taking of their pre-trial depositions.

King Albert raised his hand as if he were back in grade school.

"What was I supposed to say again, if they ask was my car moving when the crash happened?"

Nick looked up from the VCR, where he was trying to unjam the cassette of "So, You're About to Give a Deposition," a valuable tool he used in preparing his clients.

"No King, that's the whole point here. You're not supposed to say anything. All you have to do is listen to the question, then tell the truth."

King Albert looked at his wife, then back to Nick.

"The truth? Thought I was gonna be talking to lawyers."

Nick threw his hands up.

"Rene, Shlomi...will one of you set this damn machine up for me. I don't even know where things get plugged in anymore."

Nick turned to the Alonsos. "When the lawyers on the other side ask if your own lawyer told you what to say, you say 'he told me to tell the truth.'"

Shlomi gave the cassette a few light tugs.

"I can't get it out either," he said.

Rene took over. In ten seconds she had it unloosened, rewound and ready to play.

"I'm mechanically inclined," she said.

Nick hit the play button and the tape rolled.

Shlomi and Rene sat with their yellow pads before them, pens at the ready. They'd be getting an education too.

Catchy music formed a background for "flash aheads" of scenes and narration that would be shown on the tape. Then the scene changed to an attorney's office, with lawyers facing each other on either side of a table. There was a court reporter, with her steno machine and fingers going full out, and a diminutive lady client who was sitting close to her lawyer and was being grilled by a heavyset male lawyer on the other side.

King Albert's shoulders stooped; he looked like he was shivering.

"Remember," the narrator's deep voice said, "everything you say is being taken down by the court reporter—and it's for the record."

In the next scene, a lawyer asks a husband in a divorce case a series of leading questions. The man is so intimidated by the whole process that he agrees with every question, even though the opposite is the truth.

"...don't let the attorney put words in your mouth..."

After that an angry woman in a fraud case screams at a lawyer, calling him a stupid shyster for even thinking that she would misappropriate the insurance proceeds of her elderly aunt.

"...never argue with the attorney or lose your temper. You can't win an argument where the other side gets to ask all the questions and all you do is answer..."

Nick pressed the stop button and the screen turned to snow.

"This next one's my favorite," he said. "My pet peeve is when a client volunteers information to opposing counsel when they haven't been asked to."

King Albert and Muriel looked at each other, with the same confused stares.

The scene involved a personal injury case, an intersection car accident where the woman plaintiff was hit from the side after proceeding from a Stop sign. The lawyer for the insurance company of the offending driver asked her a simple question: if her view was blocked when she stepped on the gas?

"I had just put the cigarette lighter back in—"

"Oh, you were smoking."

"Yes," she says, "two packs a day. But I'm trying to quit. In fact, I was on my way to the doctor when—"

"Oh, you were sick."

Now she gets nervous.

"I didn't say I was sick." She starts rubbing her face with both hands. "I...I was completely over the flu on the day of the accident—and I wasn't still on the medication—"

"Oh, you were on medication."

Nick stopped the tape.

"Do you see what's happened here," Nick said, "just because the woman volunteered information not asked of her?"

King Albert raised his hand.

"Her lawyer got all upset."

"You bet he did. All the other lawyer asked her was if anything blocked her view. Now it looks as if she was whacked out of her mind on drugs and that she caused the accident herself."

"We weren't on no drugs," King Albert said.

Nick's eyes met Rene's and Shlomi's.

"We know that King. It's just that—well, you have to listen to the questions and answer them directly, giving no other information than what's asked. Do you understand?"

No one said anything.

Nick started the tape again.

"Let's watch the rest of it," Nick said. "Maybe something will rub off."

For thirty-five minutes the video played on— through mechanics lien cases, mortgage foreclosures, more divorces and more accidents, first the wrong way to answer, then the correct. King Albert and Muriel stayed glued to the screen, nodding their heads when it appeared that a point may have hit home.

Shlomi and Rene took notes.

Nick drank three cups of coffee.

"Well?" Nick said to his clients when it was over.

Muriel spoke in a soft, quiet voice. "I still have my baby's blanket—you can smell the powder that was on him. I hold it to my face sometimes when I feel like I'm missing him."

Nick patted her arm.

"I think that's enough for today," Nick said. "You'll both do just fine at the deposition, I can tell."

Nick rose to show the Alonsos to the door.

King Albert began to clear his throat extra loud.

Nick motioned with his head for Rene and Shlomi to step outside the room. When they did, he closed the door.

"I didn't want to bring this up, Mr. Shapiro—but the roof on our house is leaking bad and it's got to be fixed."

"Have you gotten any estimates?"

"Fourteen thousand dollars."

"For a roof?"

"Less, if we use shingle rather than concrete tiles...but we likes the concrete better."

"That's a lot of money."

"The man said he'd get started for five."

Nick closed his eyes and thought for a moment. He and Marilee had it in the bank, part of the kids' college money. It was the way business had to be done in a case like this. Both Nick and King Albert knew it.

"Come by the office tomorrow afternoon," Nick said. "I'll have five thousand for you."

"God bless you, Mr. Shapiro."

"I hope God blesses us all, King."

Rene stuck her head in Nick's office door.

"What was that all about with the Alonsos?"

"Come in," Nick said. "Close the door."

Rene sat.

"I can't lose this case, Rene. If I do, it'll break me."

"You know how to make money at this game, you'll survive."

"I don't mean financially. My spirit will be dead, dried up like a toad that ate rat poison by mistake."

"Maybe there's something I can do to keep up your spirits."

"Like deposit a fast ten thousand in my bank account?"

"I had something else in mind."

"I've got to concentrate on the case."

"Nick, you know the Alonsos didn't understand a damn thing you were trying to tell them about preparing for their testimony. That pack of lawyers will make them look like fools."

"That's exactly what I'm hoping for. Juries have a way of taking their own revenge against bullies."

Without knocking, Carol opened the door and came in.

"I'm not disturbing anything, am I?"

"Why would you be?" Nick said.

Carol gave Rene a look that an angry parent gives to a child. Then she directed her attention to Nick.

"Barbara Irati's on the phone, line one. She needs to get more of her things from the house."

"She was there a couple of weeks ago," Nick said.

"How much can you take in a compact car?"

Nick sighed.

"I'm up to my neck right now. Rene, can you handle this for me? You know the drill."

"I call her husband's lawyer," Rene said, "make the arrangements for her to be at the house when the brother is there to supervise—why doesn't this woman get a life?"

Carol moved closer to Rene.

"Maybe the poor thing's afraid the guy will kill her—he's threatened to."

Rene yawned.

"They all do—or take the kids and run off to Afghanistan—"

"Iran," Nick said.

"Wherever—it's all just another form of male abuse, trying to dominate women. Women need to start standing up for themselves."

"Get on it, will you please?" Nick said.

Rene and Carol let Nick go back to work. They stood out in the secretarial area, next to Carol's desk.

Carol's hands were on her hips. "You were trying to make a move on Nick, weren't you?" Carol said.

"You and I aren't married to each other."

"Doesn't our relationship mean anything to you?"

"If you can't handle the way I lead my life, Carol, I suggest we call it quits."

Carol held her own arms.

"No...no. I've been dumped too many times."

"By men."

"I love you, Rene—more than I've ever loved any man."

"I've got to go now, Carol—Barbara Irati waits, remember?"

CHAPTER 23

At 11:00 a.m. Thursday morning, Marilee Shapiro opened the front door of the house, still wearing a maroon cotton bathrobe. Her hair was pinned up, eyes puffy from too much sleep. She reached into the mail box by the side of the door and removed its contents. She took it all back inside, to the kitchen table, where her first cup of morning coffee awaited.

The mail was separated into piles: bills, bank statements, advertisements and junk mail. A small box wrapped in brown shopping bag paper, with no return address, was placed on the table by itself.

Marilee tore off the paper. It was an unmarked video cassette. She ran to the media room, put the cassette in the VCR, and watched.

It was her going down on Richard Greeson.

A gift from Jerry Dockett.

At 2:00 p.m. the door to Richard Greeson's townhouse swung open. He was still wearing his suit pants after rushing home from the office, but had put on a velvet smoking jacket, complete with a red silk handkerchief in the front pocket.

"You were lucky to catch me when you did,"

he said to Marilee. "I was about to leave work for the golf course."

Marilee pushed past him without saying anything until she was inside, door closed.

"Don't flatter yourself, Richard. It's not like I had to have you or die...and take off that silly jacket, you look like a slimeball from an old B movie."

He left the jacket on.

"Why so angry? I thought you wanted to—"

"I've got something else for you to think about this time, loverboy."

Marilee took the cassette from her purse.

Greeson raised an eyebrow.

"A movie—porno perhaps?"

"The best ever made," Marilee said.

"Let's watch."

After turning on the equipment, Greeson sat on the sofa in front of the T.V.

Marilee sat a few feet away from him.

"My God!" Greeson said. "It's us."

Marilee turned to him. "I'm being blackmailed."

"Let's watch more."

"Turn that goddamn thing off and talk to me."

Greeson used the remote to mute the sound, but left the video going.

"I'll bet it's my neighbor across the parking lot," Greeson said. "The guy's a fag. He got mad when he hit on me and I rejected him."

Marilee grabbed the remote from his hand and turned the TV off.

"I thought you were supposed to be a smart man," she said. "It's Jerry Dockett who's the blackmailer, a private investigator who works for my husband."

"Dockett? I know him. The bastard's probably going to blackmail me, too."

"You?"

"If Nick finds out about us, he'd have me killed," Greeson said. "That gives Dockett leverage."

"If Nick found out about us, he'd kill you himself."

Greeson felt his sweaty palms with his fingertips.

"But this isn't about you, Richard. It's the Alonso case, the big money after I dump Nick."

"Thank God it doesn't concern me."

"Well, what the hell do I do? You're my attorney."

"Technically, I'm not your—"

"Cut the crap, Richard. Help me."

Greeson took Marilee's hands; they trembled. He pulled her in against him, kissed her on the mouth, and then slid his hand inside her bra.

"I'll help you, Marilee."

Nick was at his desk, buried in a stack of papers.

Carol Emry came in, holding a phone message.

"Are you sitting down?" she said.

Nick looked up.

"No, I'm buck-broncing the Graf Zeppelin."

"Judge Porter's judicial assistant just called— he wants all the attorneys on the Alonso case in his office at two this afternoon, a status conference."

Nick's blood began to pound. The bran muffin and banana half he'd eaten for breakfast churned and sent up vapors.

"On three-hours notice?"

"Judge's secretary asked if you had any vacation plans for the week after next."

Nick put his hands together as if praying to the ceiling.

"A trial date!" he said.

"Or just a status conference."

"Judge Porter's a corrupt old dog. I've seen this tactic by him before. He went through his files, culled out the big cases to see which ones he could turn into hay for himself. He's going to push this case to trial, maybe get bought off by the defense if he gives them a continuance—or by me if we get a fast trial date."

"You'd pay a judge a bribe?"

"Never. But I'd play his game, make him think I would. Then later I'd tell him where to stick it."

"You'd never stand a chance in front of him again."

"After the Alonso case is over, I wouldn't care."

"How can you possibly be ready for trial in two weeks?"

"Carol, my dear, I've been ready for this trial for the last twenty-five years."

Nick parked close to the courthouse, in the seven dollar lot, where his opponents always parked and charged it off to their clients.

The pretty lady in the bikini had moved her hot dog stand across the street from the courthouse. Nick eyed her as he walked by. Three months before he was thinking about quitting law and buying a franchise from her. Now he had his own franchise, the Alonso case.

"Mr. Shapiro," the woman said. Her chest jiggled from one side of the cart to the other when she moved to wave to Nick. "I still have your card, you never called me."

"I eat only kosher hot dogs now," Nick said.

She seemed to pout. "Well, keep me in mind."

"I always do."

Nick waved good-bye with a tip of his briefcase. He crossed the street. The high bank of steps leading up to the courthouse seemed like an escalator to the lobby. Even the elevator was waiting for him. It was his day, he could feel it.

Nick exited on the fourth floor, and turned right at the sign that pointed to Judge Chester Porter's chambers.

A huddle of blue-suited, black wing tipped lawyers blocked the door. Their hands waved in the air, heads moved from side to side, and they spoke too fast and too loud for lawyers from blue-chip firms. There were eight of them, two from each of the four major defence firms.

Nick felt like a bowling ball approaching the pins, only this time the pins were stuck to the floorboards with superglue on shoe leather.

"There's Shapiro," a voice said from the huddle.

Randall Hunter, senior trial counsel from Simms & Malone, the firm representing the car seat manufacturer, stepped forward. He was ten years younger than Nick, but made hundreds of thousands more per year.

"Hello, Neal. It's been a while. What case was it? A whiplash, wasn't it?"

The lawyer's face was cut like Dick Tracy's, complete with a full head of blond hair. He laughed out loud.

Nick nodded. "Randall—gentlemen. It would seem I'm a bit outnumbered here."

"Your choice, old boy," Hunter said. "Our clients aren't happy with you for bringing this frivolous case against them—it makes bad publicity."

"A baby's dead and you call it frivolous?"

The lawyers formed two distinct ranks in front of Nick, Hunter at the fore.

"The van driver and the child's own parents

are the only ones responsible, Neal," Hunter said. "This case is an obvious grope for a financial deep pocket."

Nick set down his briefcase on the floor, then took a step closer to Hunter so that he stood only inches away.

"And I'm going to dig deep into those pockets, Hunter."

Hunter's face reddened. He gave a nervous laugh to release steam.

"So what's this status conference all about, Neal?" Hunter said.

"Between the eight of you, you couldn't figure it out?"

"It must concern the several motions to compel our discovery responses."

"I don't care about that anymore. I've got the evidence I need. We'll let the jury hear how you stonewalled all our requests. Now why would such innocent defendants not want to produce a few innocuous documents?"

"You won't get away with it, Shapiro."

The door to the judge's anteroom opened, bumping the backs of the second rank of lawyers. They were pushed forward by the force.

"Judge is ready for you now," Olga Gladbush, who was Judge Porter's judicial assistant for the past twenty years, said.

The blue suits pushed in ahead of Nick. They sat in the order of their importance, with Hunter at the front of the judge's conference table. One seat was left open across the table for Nick, who finally managed to make his way to it.

There was the sound of a toilet flushing. Judge Porter came out of his small bathroom on the side of the room, still zipping up his pants.

"Remain seated," the judge said. He took his

seat behind the desk at the head of the table. "There're so many of you in here it might create a wind storm with all that movement. Alonso versus Ibis Motor Corporation, etal." The thick court file was before the judge.

"Randall Hunter for Ibis Motors, Your Honor—"

"I know who you are, Mr. Hunter—and didn't they ever tell you over there at Simms & Malone that it's rude to interrupt a judge? Especially the one who's going to preside over your case?"

Hunter's face turned its peculiar brand of deep red.

"Sorry, Your Honor."

The judge, a former golf hustler who went to law school on his winnings, turned to Nick. He opened a palm that could still hit a golf ball 250 yards down the middle.

"Mr. Shapiro, you must feel like General Custer at the Last Stand."

Nick stifled a laugh. "Thank goodness these boys don't shoot arrows."

Porter's elbows were on the desk, fingertips touching. He smiled.

"I asked you all here to see where this battle was going, and to tell you that a month-long case previously before me has settled. That leaves me something very precious on my hands, gentlemen—time."

"May I speak now, Your Honor?" Hunter said.

"All right, Mr. Hunter."

"We anticipate another nine to fourteen months preparation for trial—expert witnesses, exhibits, depositions all over the country—"

"Two weeks," Judge Porter said.

"No, Your Honor, the trial will take at least three weeks."

The judge's red hair, now mostly white, seemed

to stand up a bit on its own.

"I mean, Mr. Hunter, you're going to trial in two weeks."

Hunter's face met his comrades; lips stiffened.

"It's simply not possible, Judge."

"You're being rude again, Mr. Hunter." Judge Porter looked to Nick. "Is the plaintiff ready to proceed?"

"We're ready, Your Honor."

Porter opened his hands.

"There, you see? If the plaintiff is ready, then surely the defense must be ready. There are— what—eight of you? Mr. Shapiro has to prepare essentially eight different cases. Each of you need prepare only one."

Crosstalk buzzed the room.

"Our clients will be severely prejudiced, Judge—"

Porter leaned out over his desk.

"Didn't they teach it to you in law school, Mr. Hunter?"

"Teach what, Your Honor?"

"That there's nothing like a trial date to get a case resolved?"

Porter's eyes met Nick's.

No truer words were ever sent down from the bench—and Nick knew exactly what they meant.

CHAPTER 24

It was Nick's only fear in the practice of law: beginning a jury trial first thing Monday morning. There was little or no sleep the entire weekend—the heartstopping panic when it was discovered that something that should have been done months before was still hanging fire.

Then there was always that moment, late Sunday night, when all the files and cases and depositions were packed away in briefcases, and Nick could relax and reflect—only to wake up at 3a.m. in a sticky sweat, wondering how he was going to lay a proper foundation for a crucial piece of evidence. The objections of opposing counsel would ring in his head where sleep should have been.

Dawn would finally break. There was the lonely drive to the courthouse. Sitting by himself at counsel table, Nick would wait for the bailiff to bring in the jury panel. There was a silence at that time, like before the first shot fired in a war—the brief moment of pure terror. Then he would stand, face the jury and say, "Good morning, ladies and gentlemen. My name is Neal Shapiro, and I represent...."

It was a business then, win or lose—on to the next case.

This Monday morning was different. This was the Alonso case. There could be no loss, for there would be no tomorrow.

Nick sat at the end of the table closest to the jury box. To his left was King Albert Alonso, looking confused, his eyes bloodshot. Next to him was his wife Muriel, a constant low sob on her lips, holding her dead baby's blanket, sniffing it occasionally. Then there was Rene, in a well-fitted business suit. Last was Shlomi, as out of place in his beard and skull cap as a priest in a topless bar.

The three defense tables it took to house all of the opposing attorneys crowded in on them. The case had been assigned the largest courtroom in the Harris County Courthouse, but now even it looked cramped, the blue suits and wingtips rubbing arms with the common man.

Even with all those lawyers in the courtroom, there was silence. The defense attorneys had also harbored the Monday-morning fear, and had the same puffy eyes from lack of sleep as Nick did.

A door opened from behind the high judicial bench. The judge in flowing black robes entered the room.

"All rise," the bailiff's voice echoed, "the Harris County Circuit Court is now in session. The Honorable Chester Porter presiding."

The judge took his chair.

"Please be seated," Porter said, deep voice in command. "This is Alonso versus Ibis Motors, etal. Bailiff, bring in the jury panel."

The uniformed bailiff, silver metal plates on the tips of his cowboy boots shining, guided in the fourteen plumbers, maids, school teachers, and racists—both white and black—leading them like a string of sickly birthday party ponies.

Judge Porter called out their names from a list. "Mr. James Kirkpatrick, raise your hand please."

A man in his thirties, dressed in dirty jeans and wearing weekend stubble on his face, held up an arm that looked too short for his paunchy body.

"Would you take the first seat in the top row, please?"

Nick wrote down the man's name. All rednecks would be peremptorily challenged.

Fourteen strangers sat silently: nine blacks, four whites and one Oriental. Only six of them would be selected.

After a half hour of preliminaries by the judge— name, occupation, marital status of each, Porter turned to Nick.

"You may conduct your *voir dire*, Mr. Shapiro— but I caution you to refrain from covering the same ground, and you'll remember not to get in the jury box. I don't like that. Proceed."

Nick rose to the lectern, placed his legal pad on it, then stepped to the side.

"Good morning, ladies and gentlemen. My name is Neal Shapiro. I represent King Albert Alonso and his wife Muriel. We're here because their infant son, Calvin, was killed by the negligence of the defendants." Nick gestured to the gaggle of defense lawyers. "At this point, under the rules, I'm not permitted to tell you any more details of the case, but—"

Randall Hunter rose from his seat, tall, handsome and gym-muscled. "Objection, Your Honor. Counsel is already arguing, and we haven't even started the case yet. It would be highly—"

Judge Porter's voice had the shrillness of one who had sunk a forty-foot putt for eagle.

"Sit down, Mr. Hunter and kindly do not interrupt. You'll get your chance in due course."

Two overweight black women jurors in the first row looked at each other and laughed the way black people do when whites do something dumb.

Nick continued.

"Thank you, Your Honor. Now, ladies and gentlemen, to the business at hand. We have to find out who amongst you can sit fairly and impartially in this case, whose life experiences are such that there isn't something that would prevent a fair decision for the parties in this case. To do this, I must ask you questions about yourself, not to pry or embarrass, but simply to seek the truth." Nick looked to his notes, then back at the panel. "Mr. Kirkpatrick, I understand that you're a plumber...."

Four and a half hours later, including forty-five minutes for lunch, Nick had asked every question that had ever been asked in jury *voir dire* since the English Common Law had been brought to America. It was an old plaintiff's trick: filibuster, until the other side had nothing left to say. The potential jurors had already bonded with the plaintiff's cause, so the defense could never catch up. Any attempt would seem like obvious pandering.

Hunter rose from the defense table.

"May we approach the bench for sidebar, Your Honor?"

"You may."

The defense horde followed Hunter to the far side of the judge's bench, out of the jury's earshot.

Nick had to pick his way through them.

"From now on," the judge said, "when there's a sidebar, only lead counsel of both parties will attend. This pack of lawyers is ridiculous."

A sort of frown appeared on Hunter's lips.

"That's precisely the problem, Your Honor,"

Hunter said. "Each of the eight defendants must be allowed a chance at *voir dire* and to attend sidebar—"

"You're being rude again, Mr. Hunter. I've already warned you about that twice. The next time, make sure you have your toothbrush with you; I'll find you in contempt and put you up at the Graybar Motel for the night."

Porter waited a sufficient amount of time to see the red color burn through on Hunter's Ivy League cheeks.

"I'm the captain of this ship, Mr. Hunter. What I say is the law. If you don't like it, you can appeal me."

"I don't mean to be contentious—"

"Then don't be. One lawyer per side for sidebars. Each lawyer will be able to ask questions on *voir dire*, provided the questions have not already been asked."

"But Shapiro has already asked all the questions."

"Then you've answered your own question, haven't you, Mr. Hunter?"

An hour later six jurors were sworn in, pledging on their oath to listen only to the evidence that came from the witness stand, and to render a fair and impartial verdict based on the law given to them by the judge, so help them God. They were six women, four of them black, two of them white, all of them mothers.

Judge Porter looked at his watch and spoke down from the bench.

"Each side will have one hour for opening statement, although I doubt you'll need that much time. That'll take us up to the five o'clock hour tomorrow plaintiff can present the first witness."

Hunter stood, slowly, his shoulders stooped.

"Your Honor, we'll need some time to prepare for opening."

"If you're not ready by now, you'll never be." The judge's stare seemed to drift across the room to Nick for too long. "You'll have fifteen minutes to prepare your notes; Mr. Shapiro will lead off."

Porter slammed his gavel, then exited the door behind the bench before the bailiff could order the assemblage to rise for the recess.

Nick huddled at plaintiff's table with Rene and Shlomi.

"Are you ready for opening?" Rene said to Nick. "I was hoping the judge would put it off until tomorrow morning—to give us more time."

"Porter's pushing this case down their throats," Nick said. "Look at those lawyers—they're not preparing for opening statements, they're talking with their insurance adjusters about the jury. They're going to get hammered and they know it, no matter what kind of case we put on."

The insurance adjusters for the defendants had been sitting in the audience. They took notes. If it was going badly for them, they authorized settlements. If their lawyers were scoring points, they let it ride. Their worst fear: being hit with a megamillion dollar verdict that they could have avoided had they offered a fair settlement for less.

Randall Hunter slapped his note pad and pointed to his files. If the case were to be settled now, his firm would miss out on weeks of big fees. But the adjuster folded his arms, shook his head and whispered a number to Hunter.

The other seven adjusters did the same with their attorneys.

Judge Porter's legal assistant came into the

courtroom. She handed Nick a telephone message, then left without saying anything.

Nick gave the message to Rene.

"It's from Barbara Irati," he said. "She needs to set up another safe trip to the house to get some things. I can't be bothered with that now, handle it for me, Rene."

"No problem."

Rene put the message in her purse.

Shlomi tapped Nick on the shoulder.

"Look, all the lawyers are coming this way."

Hunter stood before Nick, at the head of his entourage.

Nick stood to face Hunter.

"I'm totally against this, Shapiro," Hunter said, "but I have been...I have been authorized by my client, as have the other seven defendants, to make you an offer of settlement of one million dollars each. If you don't accept it now, the offer is withdrawn, and we'll proceed with the trial."

Nick looked to King Albert and Muriel.

"What do you think?" Nick said to his clients. "Is eight million dollars enough?"

"Whatever you think, Mr. Shapiro." King Alonso said.

Nick had never been good at math, but he could calculate in his head forty percent of any amount. He had just earned a fee of $3,200,000.

But there was no celebration, there could be no gloating over money earned at the death of a child. The finality of it all—the death and the money—saddened Nick somehow.

He never thought he'd feel that way.

PART II

CHAPTER 25

Barbara Irati pulled her station wagon to a stop at the corner and stared at her house from a half-block away. Her friend, the karate instructor, had to teach a class and couldn't come with her this time to get the last of her and Andy's things. Nick had warned her repeatedly about not going without him. She had most of what she needed, but Andy just couldn't go another weekend without her bike.

Nick Shapiro's voice reverberated in her head: she wasn't to go to the house without an escort.

Barbara smiled at the thought of Andy's joy when she saw her bike.

She stepped on the gas, then coasted to a stop at the curb in front of the house. It looked different somehow, after not being there for so long, as if she had never lived there.

She put her key in the front door lock, opened it and entered.

The only light indoors was coming in from the outside. Suddenly, the light was blocked out by the swift kick of a foot against the door, slamming it shut.

"Whore!" her husband, Saleem, screamed inches from her face. His breath was hot, bits of wetness flying out at her.

Barbara screamed.

"You're not supposed to be here." Her voice was shrill, gaspy.

He grabbed her by her long blond hair, twisted her around, then threw her down on her back onto the floor.

"The lawyers are as stupid as you."

He took a pair of handcuffs from his back pocket, put one cuff around Barbara's wrist, the other on the thin leg of the coffee table.

Saleem seemed confused. He stopped what he was doing, then he began looking around the room as though for instructions for what came next.

He went to the coffee table, where his checklist was written on a piece of Andy's school notebook paper: "One, lock the door; two, check the gun for bullets...."

It gave Barbara time to raise the table leg and slip the handcuff underneath. She hesitated a second, making sure Saleem was not looking, then she was on her feet, at the door, turning the deadbolt—then on the outside steps.

"Come back," Saleem shouted from the doorway.

Barbara screamed again. This time neighbors, who were out doing Saturday-morning lawn mowing and house painting, looked up.

She made it to the sidewalk.

Saleem raised the three-inch .357 magnum pistol, took aim and fired from ten feet.

The bullet tore through Barbara's left shoulder blade, sending her to the grass, on her back, bleeding.

Saleem walked down the steps, stood over his wife with the gun pointed down at her.

"You can never leave me!"

Barbara's lips trembled. Without words, she pleaded for her life.

Saleem pressed the gun barrel between her breasts and fired.

Barbara's body recoiled.

He looked to the sky for a moment, then bent at the waist and picked her head up by her hair. He fired two more shots pointblank. One, sideways, took out both eyes. The second left Barbara's nose hanging off the side of her cheek, giving her once pretty face the inhuman look found only in a horror movie.

The neighbors who had witnessed the murder from next door and across the street stood motionless, themselves frightened.

Saleem went back inside the house, read his checklist again. In seconds, he appeared in the doorway. Gun in hand, he walked past his wife's mangled figure and sat under a small shade tree in the front yard.

He put the barrel of the gun in his mouth and fired.

CHAPTER 26

The telephone rang at nine o'clock Sunday morning. Nick and Marilee had celebrated his victory in the Alonso case the night before at Branden's Restaurant, on the river. Nick did most of the celebrating. His head, still thick with the aftereffects of the drinks, pounded into the pillow with each ring.

"It's for you," Marilee said, "a client I think."

Her words were part of a dream Nick was having. It took time for them to register as being real.

"What do they want?" Nick groaned.

"It's a woman. What do they ever want?"

Marilee got out of bed and went to the bathroom. She was going to tell Nick about the divorce at Branden's last night, but she was having too good a time. She would tell him today, then be in Richard Greeson's office to prepare the papers Monday morning.

"Hello?" Nick's voice was craggy with a combination of sleep and hangover.

"Is this Mr. Shapiro?"

Nick didn't answer.

"My name is Nora Federsberg—Barbara Irati's aunt?"

"I'll be in the office tomorrow around noon—"

"Barbara's husband shot her dead yesterday, then killed himself." The accent was southern, the words sadly matter of fact.

Nick came awake. He turned over and sat up, tangling himself in the phone cord.

"I don't—"

"She was going back to the house to get some things. The police detective says Saleem was going to torture her before he killed her—had a checklist of what he was going to do to her."

Nick's headache concentrated in a shaft directly behind his left eye, all the way back through his brain. His stomach reeled.

"She was not supposed to be there alone—my God—"

"The police notified us last night, my husband and I flew in...saw your name on some papers in her purse, about the divorce."

Why were they calling him? The poor girl.

"There was supposed to be a deposition in my office at the end of the week. I was going to take her husband's testimony—"

"Police think he'd have killed her in your office if he hadn't found her in the house. Probably have shot you and your staff, too. We don't know what to do next, Mr. Shapiro—the house, the money and the other property—Andy."

"Can you see me in the office first thing in the morning?" Nick said. "I'll try to answer your questions then."

"We'll be there, Mr. Shapiro."

"And, Mrs. Federsberg, I'm so sorry about your niece—she was such a sweet person."

"They don't come any better."

Nick was already dressed when Marilee emerged from the bathroom wearing only sexy panties and a Wonder Bra.

"Neal, we need to talk, now."

"A client of mine has just been murdered by her husband. I don't have time to talk."

"Look here, Neal. Clients come and go; I have something to say."

Nick brushed her aside, made it to the dresser and put on his wristwatch. "I'm going out, need to find Rene, get to the bottom of this."

Marilee tried to block the doorway, but stepped aside when she saw Nick wasn't slowing down.

"On a Sunday morning a man doesn't talk to a woman who isn't his wife—unless it's about schtupping her."

Nick stopped in the hallway and turned around.

"How would you know about that, Marilee? Didn't you hear anything I just said?"

"You haven't heard anything I've said for the last twenty-five years. All right, go to the whore. It doesn't make any difference anymore. I'll tell you what I have to say when you get back."

"*If* I come back. I may kill Rene. You can talk to me in jail, after I'm arrested."

Nick ran out of the house, slamming the front door too hard. The noise woke Tommy, who had come out into the hallway from his bedroom.

"Where did Dad go?" The sleepy-eyed boy was holding a pillow across his chest.

"To see a woman about a murder. Go back to sleep."

"When's he coming home? He was going to show me how to play golf today."

"As far as I'm concerned, your father doesn't have to come home ever again."

Nick pounded on the door until his fist hurt. "Open up, Rene!"

An eye appeared in the peephole, red as Nick's own.

"Nick?"

Rene opened the door slowly and looked both ways down the apartment hallway, as if she didn't want the neighbors to connect the noise with her.

Nick steamed past her, into the living room. He didn't even bother looking through her sheer negligee, which showed everything.

"I can't get you to take me to dinner," Rene said, "and now you practically break into my house on a Sunday morning to see me. Have a fight with your wife?"

She closed the door.

"Barbara Irati was murdered by her husband at their house," Nick said. His lips narrowed.

If the words registered, Rene pretended otherwise. "How awful—we all knew the guy was a nut."

Nick grabbed a handful of Rene's hair, pulling her into him with a jerk.

"What did you do with the phone message Judge Porter's secretary gave me in the courtroom?"

Rene didn't try to free herself from Nick's grip. She even smiled a little at the pain.

"I took care of it, Nick, just as you asked—set up the appointment at the house with her husband's lawyer, she arranged for her bodyguard friend again, the whole thing."

Nick looked around, saw Rene's purse on the pass-through bar near the kitchen. He dragged her across the room by her hair to the purse and opened it with his free hand.

"What the fuck is this?" he said, holding the message out for Rene to see.

"I called, Nick, honest."

"Bullshit."

He pushed the message hard into her face, then slapped her across the cheek with his open hand.

"You're responsible for that girl's death."

Nick slapped her again.

"I like it rough," Rene said.

"I could kill you."

"Go easy. I didn't say I made the calls directly. I instructed Carol to do it. If she messed up—"

"And Barbara's still dead." Nick thought for a moment. "Get dressed, you're coming with me to Carol's, now."

"Want to watch us?"

"I want to strangle you, but you've got a reprieve until after I hear what Carol has to say."

"Did you ever do that, Nick—choke a woman during sex? They say it's supposed to be a real rush, to take the first breath, just when you come. It lasts forever."

Nick wanted to beat her up right there, give her what she was asking for.

"You've got five minutes to get ready, or I take you just as you are."

"Promise?"

Rene made certain her bedroom door was closed tightly before she dialed Carol's number.

"Sunday morning's the only time I get to sleep," Carol said on the other end of the line, drowsy. "I always like to hear your sweet voice, but now?"

"Something's come up. Nick's here, and—"

"Nick?"

"He's on drugs or something...wants to get in my pants I think."

"Can I help?"

"That's why I'm calling. I figure the only way to get him off my back is to take him over to your place. Maybe he'll settle down a bit by then."

"Or maybe he'll try to do us both."

"Would you mind?'

"Not if I can have you to myself, after."

"Sweet. And there's something you can do for me."

"Umm humm...."

"There's been an accident. Barbara Irati and her husband reconciled last week—she had moved back into the house, he was cleaning a gun when it went off and killed her."

"God, no—"

"Yeah. Anyhow Nick's got this crazy idea that I had something to do with it; so when we get to your place could you just tell him that you called Barbara on Friday and she told you everything was all right? It'll make Nick feel better—I think he liked her."

"Anything you want, Rene."

"And, Carol, pretend like you didn't know we were coming, I don't want Nick to think we're trying to patronize him."

"Don't worry. All I can think about is that poor girl...and you."

Carol lived in a neighborhood of three-bedroom crackerbox houses that was once nice, but now had junk cars in the front yards and iron burglar bars on the windows. The house was a legacy of her divorce. She had stayed in it too long, prices had dropped, and now it was impossible for her to move.

Nick cruised down the street trying to read broken address numbers.

"I should have brought my gun," Rene said.

"Just keep your mouth shut and let me question Carol. I'll get to the bottom of this, fast."

"Whatever you want, boss."

Carol greeted them at the door with a smile, then checked herself.

Rene positioned herself behind Nick on the stoop and made a silent "shhhh" with her lips.

"This is quite a surprise," Carol said. She opened the door and let them in.

Nick stood directly in front of her.

"I'll get right to it," he said. "Did you call Barbara Irati on Friday?"

Carol looked to Rene before answering, remembered their phone conversation.

"She said everything was all right."

"Did you make the arrangements?"

Carol hesitated a moment. "Certainly I did. Why, what are you trying to get at?"

"Barbara was shot and killed by her husband, then he killed himself."

Carol looked confused. "But why would he kill himself?"

"Because he couldn't face prison, couldn't live with himself for taking the life of his daughter's mother—why do you think he goddamn did it?"

Carol dropped her head on Nick's shoulder.

"But it was all just an accident, Nick. You can't blame anyone."

"Who told you it was an accident?"

Carol's face reddened when her eyes met Rene's. "They had reconciled," Carol said, crying. "Barbara was back in the house with him."

Nick fell back into the sofa, held his head in his hands. After a while, he looked up.

"You didn't call, did you Rene? And neither did Carol."

"What's this all about?" Carol said.

Rene sat in a chair across from the sofa.

"What's the difference?" Rene said. "Barbara Irati knew the dangers; she went to the house by

herself anyway. It was no one's fault but her own—
and, of course, her asshole dead husband."

Nick yelled so loud it made the windows vi-
brate. "You don't get it, do you? She thought we
had made the arrangements for her. That's why
she went. She thought she was safe. You killed
her, Rene, you did."

"Not my fault, no way."

Carol's crying became louder.

"And you," Nick pointed an angry finger at
Carol, "you went along with her." Nick got up and
made for the door. "I'm sure you'll see to it Rene
gets back home," he said to Carol. "I wouldn't have
her in my sight ever again."

"But Nick—" Carol sobbed.

"Just give me your forwarding address, Rene.
I'll have your things delivered. Don't come near
the office, or I might not be able to control myself."

"Fuck you," Rene said.

Nick walked past Rene, as if she no longer ex-
isted.

"And as for you, Carol, maybe Rene'll hire you
at her new job. You and I are through. You're fired."

"I didn't know anything, Nick. Honest."

Nick slammed the door and drove off.

Carol sat on the sofa and wept.

Rene came to her and stroked her hair.

"No man can talk to a woman like that," Rene
said, "and get away with it."

Carol laid her head on Rene's breast, looked
into Rene's face.

"I've never seen Nick like that," she said. "He
was so upset."

"About what?" Rene said. "That his client was
killed by a madman, and he's going to be sued
because of it and lose everything he made on the
Alonso case?"

"Is that what you think?"

"He doesn't give a shit about the girl—just the money. He busted his ass his whole life for it, now it's going to be taken away."

"Hold me, Rene, just hold me tight and tell me you love me."

Rene put her arms around Carol, but looked straight across the room at the wall.

"You know I love you, Carol, more than anything."

They kissed.

"And I love you, Rene."

Rene played with Carol's hair.

"Carol, do you still have check writing privileges on Nick's office account?"

"I suppose so, why?"

"We've got to protect ourselves, when will the Alonso settlement money be in?"

"By wire, tomorrow. What does that have to do with anything?"

"We've still got our keys to the office. We know the burglar alarm code. We could go there right now, write a check to ourselves for the whole amount—"

"Steal over three million dollars from Nick?"

Rene stroked Carol's breast, with attention to a nipple that had now grown hard.

"Of course not," Rene said close to Carol's ear. "We take what our bonuses would have been if he hadn't dumped us like this, then invest the rest for him. When this Irati thing blows over, he'll get it all back, in spades."

"It's grand theft, we'd go to jail."

"Not when I explain to Nick that it would actually be the perfect way for him to hide the money from a judgment levy against him by Irati's estate. If the police think that's theft, then you and I could disappear. The bank's insurance company would eventually replace the money. Nick gets his, we get ours, and the Irati estate gets theirs."

Carol didn't respond.

Her eyes closed tightly, while Rene slid her hand inside her blouse.

"Yes, Rene. Whatever you say."

CHAPTER 27

Nick sat at his office desk, took the notebook-sized check register from the drawer and set it down before him. He used to hate paying bills, stacked them up a foot high next to the telephone for months at a time before he could write a check, even when he had the money. Now, a fifteen hundred dollar phone bill was no more painful than buying a pack of chewing gum.

Nick had no way of knowing that the night before Rene and Carol had taken a check from the back of the book and written it to themselves for $3.4 million.

The account had only $769 in it.

There was the familiar whoosh of air coming from the reception area. Glass in the office windows rattled. The wood-toned broken doorbell tried to ring out a chime, but sounded more like a bat hitting a triple.

Shlomi went from his office to the pass-through window, then to Nick's office.

"Judge Porter's here to see you," Shlomi said. His temple locks hung down in two perfect curls.

"So the cobra finally reared its ugly head," Nick said. "What did you tell the honorable judge?"

"That you were in. I tell lies only on the day before Yom Kippur."

"I never knew that trick...might as well tell the old sod I'll be right with him."

Nick finished writing a check to his auto insurance company—the first time he'd ever paid the entire premium all at once. He made a point of deducting the amount of the payment and entered the new balance in the margin. He stared at it for a while, smiled, then put the checkbook back in his desk.

He got up and went to the front door, stopping for a moment to ponder Carol's empty desk. Maybe he shouldn't have been so hard on her. He'd call her—fifteen years was too long just to throw away in a fit of anger.

"Judge Porter, what an unexpected surprise this is."

"Oh hell, Neal, we're informal here, just call me, 'Ace.'"

"Come in Judge, my office is around the corner."

They sat. Nick had left the door to his office open, but the judge closed it.

"You're about the last person I thought would walk in the door this morning, Judge."

"I thought you would have been expecting me, Neal." The red, cobwebbed veins in Porter's nose seemed to light up.

"And why might that be?"

Porter rolled his tongue inside his check. "Let's not play games with each other Shapiro—"

"I thought it was Neal, Ace."

"No need to be smart. I've been at this game a long time, survived it all—the investigations, even an indictment or two. A lot of lawyers got damn rich because of me—and they all knew how they got that way. You do know how you got yours, don't you, Neal?"

"Am I supposed to write you out a check for your services? How much?"

The judge laughed, licked his lower lip a bit.

"I can see you're new at this. Allow me to continue your legal education, if I may. You form a dummy, off-shore corporation, 'invest' $320,000 in it. Then the corporation wires certified funds to a secret bank account in the Turks and Caicos—"

"Uh huh."

"It's ten percent of the fee I got for you. That's standard."

"You get three hundred twenty thousand dollars of my money?"

"Like the sun rises every morning."

Porter's eyes narrowed, piercing Nick's own.

Nick took a yellow legal pad from his desk, put it in front of himself, as if he were going to take notes. He wrote something, then held it up to the judge.

"I'm not in the mood for jokes here," Porter said.

"In case you can't read, it says 'go fuck yourself.'"

"No, it doesn't. It says you're awfully stupid for a Jew boy. Better think about this one a little bit more, Shapiro."

"You get nothing from me. I took that case and turned it into gold—on my own. It gets shared with nobody, not even a corrupt, burned-out old asshole like you."

Porter slammed his fist on the desk.

"Those insurance companies settled with you because I forced them to!"

"That's bullshit. And I never promised you anything. Besides, it wouldn't be legal, would it Judge, for me to pay you a cut, a bribe? I could tell the Qualifications Committee you tried to shake me down."

"Lawyers with grudges pull that stunt on judges all the time. The committee's used to it. Your word against mine—and my unexpected visit didn't give you the time to wear a wire. Now, let's stop all this nonsense and get down to business, shall we?"

The two men stared at each other.

When Nick had first started practicing law his mentor, Mel Forman, who began lawyering in Harris County at a time when it had only twenty-eight attorneys, told Nick never to be greedy. Spread the wealth around, is what Mel said, live to make more another day.

Nick didn't understand what that meant then, and he didn't understand it now.

"Not even if my ability to get a hard-on in the future depended on it," Nick said. "If you're not out of here in thirty seconds, I'll pick up this phone and call the FBI. They're going to wonder why you're in my office on a Monday morning, instead of at the courthouse dispensing injustice."

Porter stood, his face redder than Santa Clause's uniform.

"I'll see to it that you never practice law in this town again, Shapiro."

Nick glanced down at his partially open desk drawer and saw his checkbook. "I won't have to, Ace."

CHAPTER 28

Nick picked up on line two by the eighth ring; he still hadn't finished the conversation with the stockbroker, had him on hold. It was impossible for one person to handle the telephones alone. How had Carol done it all those years?

"I've been waiting for you," Nick said to Nora Federsberg, Barbara Irati's aunt. "It's a very complicated situation."

There was momentary silence on the other end of the line.

"We decided to see another lawyer before we came to you, Mr. Shapiro—this afternoon—you know, to get a second opinion."

Nick looked at his watch and sighed. The Federsberg's were already an hour late for their appointment. He had things to do, financial advisors to see, his wealth had to be invested.

"This is a legal problem," Nick said, "not a medical one. Second opinions are for doctors, not lawyers. You don't need to waste your time on someone else. I want to help because I feel so badly for the situation."

"We were thinking last night..."

It was the worst thing a client could do.

"...if Barbara went to the house by mistake,

say—someone might be responsible for what happened to her."

"You can discuss that with me."

"But what if it was you, Mr. Shapiro, who made the mistake, or someone in your office? Wouldn't that be a conflict of interest for us to talk to you about it?"

The Federsbergs had already spoken with another attorney.

"Your daughter's husband is the only person responsible for her death. He was the only one who pulled the trigger—and damn it!—she didn't take her bodyguard with her. If only she had."

"But what if she was sent into a death trap by someone? Wouldn't they be negligent?"

"Not where someone's intervening criminal act takes over, like first-degree murder. Her husband could have killed her anyplace, anytime—he had that power. The police think he would have done it the next week, in my office when we were to meet for depositions."

"Saleem had threatened to kill her many times in the past. She shouldn't have been sent to the house."

It was no use. They wouldn't listen. God, Nick hated lawyers. The Federsbergs would sue him. They really had no case, for the very reason Nick had explained, but he would be forced to pay a substantial settlement, just to protect the rest of his money, case or not.

Or find a way to force Rene to pay.

Nick thought he would lose his temper, but instead his voice remained calm. "You're making a mistake, Mrs. Federsberg."

"No, Mr. Shapiro, I think you're the one who's made a mistake."

Shlomi stuck his head in Nick's doorway.

"What was that all about?" he said.

"You heard?"

"I was in the law library doing some research, couldn't help but hear."

"Have a seat."

Shlomi entered the office and took one of the chairs before Nick's desk.

"The shit is starting to hit the atomic accelerator," Nick said.

"Spic and span, little man. Where were you when the quark hit the fan?"

"Exactly. Times have changed, Shlomi. The whole country's gone lawsuit happy. Sue over anything, maybe you'll ring the bell. What's worse than the litigants are the lawyers who take on such cases. In my heyday, they'd have been run out of town on a string of barbed wire."

"When will people realize that God is the one who decides these things. If people would just concentrate on trying to do good in the world—you know, 'love thy neighbor'—God would provide."

"Tell that to Barbara Irati's aunt. She's going to sue me on behalf of the estate."

"You don't know that. You're stressed out, Nick, it creates paranoia. Without Carol to run the office, you're like a meteor hitting the earth's atmosphere at the speed of light."

"Poof."

"Still have that book on Jewish meditation I gave you?"

Nick nodded.

"Practice it now. Let your mind take you into a positive realm. Explore the good you can do for the world with your new-found wealth."

"I want to do good for me."

Shlomi stood. "Let the meditation take you to

the edge of the stars, and then beyond. Maybe you'll find the answers. Get Carol back in the office—that'll help, too."

Shlomi closed the door behind him.

Nick sat back in his chair, and tightened the blinds on his window so no direct sunlight came in. It wasn't dark, looked more like twilight, perfect to relax the mind.

He began repeating the words "master of the universe" in Hebrew. Over and over he chanted the mantra, until he fell into a trance-like state, a near sleep close to the peace that comes just before going under in a Sunday afternoon nap.

Bad thoughts came in from the sides and were bounced into infinity with no effort. The light of understanding shone bright, all was black and white. The Hebrew letters for God's name stood solid, like the rocks of Stonehenge. Nick repeated the mantra by rote, striving for more—to see into the future.

Once again he found himself at the high steps of God's court. He was pulled across the courtyard by an unknown source. The curtain to the hall of divine justice hung before him.

This time it opened.

At first nothing was visible. Then, angels lifted a gossamer veil from the judicial bench, and there sat God, the master Nick Shapiro had summoned, poised to read the verdict on his soul.

"Nick. The phone. Wake up." Shlomi's voice was calm and low, as if he were waking a child for school in the morning.

"I wasn't asleep, I—"

"I picked up your phone. There's a lawyer on hold—a Dawkins or Hawkins—about the Alonso case."

"Bobby Hawkins?" Nick came wide awake. Hawkins was a lawyer who sued other lawyers for a living.

Nick picked up the phone, cupped the speaker with his hand and waved Shlomi off.

"This is Nick Shapiro."

"Do you know me, Shapiro?"

"Sure, I know you—and I hope you haven't interfered with my clients in any way, Hawkins. You've got the reputation."

"Your clients? I'm afraid you've got it backwards, Shapiro. The Alonsos are my clients now—and guess who's the new defendant?"

The calm achieved by the meditation was quickly replaced by hot, bubbling blood—then a sick dread that Nick felt deep in his stomach.

"What's this all about?"

"You shortchanged those poor people, Shapiro. Should've taken the case to a jury, could have gotten twice as much."

"Or nothing. That's b.s. and you know it. A good settlement is always better than tossing a coin with a jury."

"The Alonsos say you pressured them into a settlement they didn't want. Forced them into it just so you could make a quick fee, at their expense. It was their child who was killed, not yours."

"The average verdict in this town is between three hundred thousand and a million for a dead infant. I got them seven times more than that."

"Only because there were multiple defendants. And because of that, you could've gotten even more."

"What did you do, you piece of dogshit, read about the case in the paper, then call my people up and pump them full of your lies?"

"No need to get emotional. You've got malpractice insurance, don't you? They'll pay us."

"A hundred thousand policy. Read it and weep, asshole."

"Plus three million something for your fee. Why not just settle for a million right now, and get this unpleasant business over with?"

"And you'd make four hundred thousand dollars on a phone call? No way. When this is over, the Alonsos will sue you. It'll never end."

"Have it your way, Shapiro. You can get out cheap now, or I'll drag you through the courts and the newspapers as the exploiter of the century—'no-good Jew lawyer dupes poor, black parents of dead baby.'"

"Ever have your nose broken, Hawkins?"

"Threats aren't effective against me. They're a way of life."

"It's no threat."

"You'll be served with suit papers by morning."

"Hawkins, lawyers like you should be put to death."

"Tut. Tut. Stop being so self-righteous. We're all the same, Shapiro. It's how we make a living. Some of us are a bit fancier than others, more politically connected, better moral facades, but when you strip us naked, we all are the same color, green."

"Not me, Hawkins."

"Oh yes, Shapiro, especially you."

Shlomi brought in a waterpitcher and a glass on a tray.

"Drink," he said to Nick. "You need it."

"Something stronger is what I need."

Shlomi sat and drank the water himself.

"How can the Alonsos do this to you, after everything you've done for them? You risked your career on their case. How can they not be satisfied with what you got for them?"

"Money, especially easy money, has a way of changing people. Makes them do what they otherwise would never dream of."

Shlomi nodded. "It's really just another form of idolatry. The very thing God keeps warning us about in the Torah. It doesn't always have to be a graven image that we bow down to."

There was the familiar suction of air at the front door, windows rattling. A man's voice, deep from within a barrel chest, called out through the empty central office.

"Nick, you in?"

It was Jerry Dockett. He stuck his thick forearm through the pass-through window and let himself in.

"I didn't know there was someone with you," Dockett said from Nick's doorway.

"It's only Shlomi. Whatever you've got to say, he can hear it too. Today, I need all the company I can find."

"I've got to talk to you about this alone, Nick."

"Mind?" Nick said to Shlomi.

Shlomi stood. "The way it's going, I'm sure I'll hear about it soon."

Dockett waited until Shlomi returned to the library before he locked Nick's office door.

"It's been bothering me all along; I can't sleep." Dockett said.

"Sit down, what?"

"Remember that night you had me follow your wife out to her real estate deal?"

Nick felt his pulse quicken. He nodded his head.

"Well, I lied to you. She was having an affair; I got it on video tape."

Dockett removed the cassette from inside his shirt and placed it on the desk.

Nick took a deep breath. "God, why didn't you tell me?"

"That's the part that's been bothering me, Nick. I was trying to blackmail your wife—for a piece of the money you made on the Alonso case—the money she'd get after she divorced you."

Nick's eyes drooped.

"So, who was she having the affair with, or are you trying to sell me a blank tape?"

"It ain't blank, Nick. It's Marilee and Richard Greeson—going at it like high school seniors on prom night."

Nick had visions of his wife and Greeson, naked, her touching him. He'd find them, come into the room from behind, without the lovers seeing, shoot them both in the head, then turn the gun on himself. What about his children? It was the Irati case all over again, in a different form.

"Why tell me now?" Nick said. "You could have made yourself a piece of change on the deal."

"Let's just say that the work you gave me on the Alonso case got my head out of the bottle at a time when no other lawyer trusted me to gas up his car. Even if I got the money from your wife, I'd probably hit the skids again—drink it all up, then piss it away."

"So you thought you'd save your liver by coming clean with me."

"It's not that, Nick. It's what I said—and I hate Greeson's guts. If there's any way you can use the tape against him, then you'd be doing us both a favor."

"Let me see the tape."

"It's not a good idea, Nick. Just take my word for it, what's on there."

Nick reached across his desk, picked up the cassette from the desk and stood. "The VCR's in the library."

"Nick?"

Nick ignored Shlomi's presence. He powered up the VCR, slid the tape in.

In full color and surround sound, the scene at Greeson's townhouse began to reenact.

"My God, Nick," Shlomi said, "that's your wife." Shlomi turned his head and covered his eyes.

"I've seen enough," Nick said. He turned and walked back to his office, an ashen-faced ghost of a man.

Dockett turned off the machine and pulled the tape. "I told him not to watch it," Dockett said to Shlomi.

Nick was in his office, sitting on the old sofa, clutching one of its pillows against his stomach.

Dockett and Shlomi came in. They sat.

"I want to kill them both," Nick said.

Shlomi held up his palms. "Don't do anything foolish, Nick."

"We can use the tape against both of them," Dockett said.

"I want to kill Marilee, but I don't want to lose her."

Nick looked up at the two men. "That makes sense, doesn't it?"

"No, Nick," Dockett said. "But I know what you mean."

Nick began to cry. "What good is all my money if I don't have my wife?"

"Maybe," Shlomi said, "if you have it in your heart to forgive her, you can patch things up. I've seen worse cases get back together."

"Any more copies of the tape?" Nick asked.

Dockett hesitated for a moment, then: "One

more, at my apartment."

"I want it—and nobody is to know about this, understand?" Nick's eyes were stringy red, like a hangover.

Both men nodded.

"I'll bring the copy by this afternoon," Dockett said.

Nick sat with his head in his hands.

"Come on," Shlomi said to Dockett, "let's leave Nick alone. He has much to think about."

On his way out the front door of the office, Dockett bumped his huge body into Milo Contraro, a fellow PI and process server.

"Thought you'd fallen off the face of the earth a long time ago," Milo said. "How long's it been?"

"I lost count. Why you here, Milo?"

"Got some suit papers to serve on Nick Shapiro. God, I love to see their faces when lawyers get sued. They take it harder than John Q. Public. Guess they know how bitter their own medicine is."

"What's it about?"

"His wife is suing him for divorce, asking for millions. Richard Greeson's representing her."

"I'll take the papers for him."

"And deprive me of one of the purest pleasures in the business? Not a chance."

Dockett grabbed the suit papers from Milo's hand. "I'll give the papers to Nick later, when he's feeling better. He's had more bad news than one man should have to suffer in a single day."

CHAPTER 29

The rocks in the hubcaps of Carol Emry's ten-year-old station wagon sounded like a child's noise grogger. The worn shocks and swaying motion at each stop light gave the rocks the final sound of the rattle coming to rest.

Heads turned as she and Rene sped off at a green light on Gables Boulevard.

"Maybe we should open up an account at a new bank," Carol said. "They won't know me there."

"That's exactly why we have to use your bank. You and Nick have the same bank; they'll give you immediate clearance of the check when it's deposited into your account."

"Won't a bank officer call Nick for verification, or something?"

"Are you getting nervous on me? They don't verify on a deposit, only when a check's cashed. It's as good as—money in the bank."

Rene laughed at what she said.

Carol lit a cigarette off the butt of her last. She reached across the seat and took Rene's hand. "Tell me again, where do we hide out if the police get involved?"

"How's your Spanish? Spain has a weak extradition treaty with the U.S. We've got enough money to spread around over there, keep people off our backs—except you Carol, my love, I want you on my back."

"You're not just saying that?"

"Of course, I'm saying it. Now look, just don't let your emotions go south on me. We've both got to remain calm, act before Nick finds out that more than three million of his dollars are missing."

"He'd kill me if he found out," Carol said.

"He'd rape you, then kill you."

"Well, if it was in that order—"

"There's the bank, get in the right lane. We won't go inside, use the drive-in window."

Carol missed the turn and had to go around the block. The rain started, fogging up the car's windows.

"Don't blow it again," Rene said. "We haven't got much time."

"I can't see anything."

After two more passes, Carol finally got in one of two open drive-through lanes.

"You picked the wrong lane," Rene said. "That guy in front of us is handing the teller a sack of business receipts—shit."

"It'll give us time to talk. I feel better when you talk to me."

Rene had been waiting for a few spare moments to discuss the rest of the plan with Carol.

"I thought of a way to protect you in all this," Rene said. "You know, if Nick doesn't like our plan about protecting his money for him."

Carol played with Rene's fingers, interlocking them with hers.

"You write a check to me for the full amount of the money, then I'll deposit it in my own account. That way, if the police get involved, you can tell them I forced you to do it at...gunpoint, duress, whatever. No sense both of us taking the rap for it."

Tears welled in Carol's eyes. "You'd do that for me, Rene?"

"Because I care about you, Carol."

The foggy windows provided perfect cover for Rene to slide over next to Carol, place a thigh between both of Carol's, and kiss her.

"They know me here," Carol said. "I don't want anyone to see us."

Rene's hand was already inside Carol's panties.

"In a little while, it won't make any difference who sees us."

Carol sat in her living room, lights off like Rene had instructed. She stood, lit a cigarette so that it was the only thing aglow in the darkened house. She paced back and forth, stopped, then held the tip of the cigarette close to her watch. It was 8:45 p.m. Rene was supposed to be there at eight—with the airline tickets to New York, then Spain.

Carol smoked and paced some more, then sat back on the couch and wept. What if Rene had gotten into an accident?

It was nine-thirty.

Carol went to her bedroom in the back of the house. She turned on a low wattage night light so she could read her personal telephone directory. Jerry Dockett's name was nearly obliterated by time and fingernail scratches. She dialed.

"Dockett." The voice sounded tired, but sober.

"Jerry, this is Carol."

"I don't know any Carol...Carol Emry?"

"It's me, Jerry. I know it's an imposition, but do you think you could come over now? I wouldn't ask if it wasn't important."

"It's getting late, I'm tired. And too much time has passed between us."

"I can't find Rene; I think she's missing, something happened to her."

"Why should you care so much about her?"

"I know things didn't end well with us...I can't talk over the phone. Jerry, it's life or death. You've got to come."

Dockett was staring at a bottle of still-sealed Old Gumshoes. It was the first bottle he'd bought in over a month. Its amber glow beckoned, and told him to tell Carol he was busy for the evening with company.

Dockett eyed the bottle again. "All right," he said. "I'll come. For old times' sake."

"Hurry."

He'd never heard Carol's voice sound as desperate as that before.

Dockett strapped his five-shot, .38 police special to his ankle and got in his van.

"Had trouble finding your house with the lights off like that," Dockett said to Carol Emry. "What gives? Did you rob a bank?"

Carol looked up and down the street before she closed the door behind him.

"I think Rene's been kidnapped, maybe murdered, you've got—"

"Hey, hey, would you slow down? No kiss, even on the cheek? You're talking about Rene from Nick's office, right?"

Carol grabbed Dockett by the hand and pulled him to the couch. She could just barely get her hand around two of his fingers.

Carol chewed at her nails. "Rene was supposed to meet me here at eight, she didn't call—"

"Why would anybody want to kill her, and why

was she supposed to meet you here tonight?"

"You sound like a cop."

"I am—was. Isn't that why you called me?"

"Do you have to ask so many questions?"

"That's what cops do."

Carol lit a smoke and offered one to Dockett. He took it. Carol's eyes searched the corner of the ceiling for a moment.

"Rene and I have become...friendly, in the office. Good friends, actually. We were supposed to go out to dinner tonight, talk about a case she's handling for Nick—and when she didn't come to pick me up, well, naturally, I became worried. I thought maybe you could use your police scanners, call the hospitals—whatever it is you guys do to find somebody who's missing."

Dockett took a long drag off his cigarette and wished he'd taken the bottle with him.

"You're lying to me."

"No, I'm not."

"Nick canned both you and Rene over the Irati murder. You think I don't know? Besides, you never could tell a very good lie—you smile funny while you're saying it, like a pitcher telegraphing his curve. Now stop bullshitting me, or I'm gone. Got a date waiting back at my apartment."

"Is she pretty?"

"Amber hair."

Carol looked Dockett in the face for a moment, then burst into tears. She buried her head in his chest and sobbed away like a sixteen-year-old who had just been stood up by the homecoming king.

Dockett stroked her hair. He'd always liked the way her hair smelled. "What is it, Carol?" His voice was deep but gentle.

Carol looked up, still crying.

"We stole Nick's money from the Alonso case,

Rene and me. Almost three and a half million."

"Are you on drugs?"

"If only I were, something real strong."

Dockett took Carol by the shoulders and sat her up.

"How could you steal Nick's money?"

Carol kept sniffling. "Rene said we'd really be protecting the money for him—from Irati's estate—that we'd just take the interest as what he owed us as a sort of severance pay, give him back the principal."

"You believed that?"

"I wanted to, even after Rene had me write a check from my account to hers for the full amount."

"Oh, brother."

"Now Rene's gone."

"What did you think she was going to do with the money, buy you a prince on a white horse to whisk you away?"

"Something like that."

"Christ. She could be anywhere in the world right now. With that kind of dough, she could hire the space shuttle to take her to Mars. My God, how could you be so stupid?"

"I didn't do it for money," Carol screamed. "I did it for love. Rene and I were having an affair."

At first Dockett wanted to make a joke. He stood slowly, standing over Carol.

"You dropped me for another woman?"

"No, Jerry. You and I broke up because you were an alcoholic. I tried—but as much as I loved you, you loved the booze more. Rene came along after the fact."

"So you turned to women?"

"Rene conned me in more ways than one."

Dockett wanted to head for the door; he felt queazy in the stomach. But he stayed.

"She mentioned something about Spain—no extradition treaty?"

"Does Nick know anything yet?"

"No."

"If I can find Rene at the airport, maybe he won't have to know anything. If not—"

"Do this for me, Jerry, and I may even learn to love you again."

Dockett kissed her cheek, smelled her hair, remembered.

"Stay put. I've got some work to do. As the lawyers say, time is of the essence."

CHAPTER 30

Nick strode up the sidewalk to the front door of his office. Despite the problems that had smacked him in the face the day before, he was whistling and singing a tune from the sixties. "Rhona's little girl, fickle little girl, you didn't want him when he wanted youoooooo...." The melody was wry, kind of like salsa sauce, sour and hot, easy to repeat. He picked up the morning copy of the *Preview*, still whistling. After all, he still had his money.

The suction of the front door rattled the windows. It distracted Shlomi, who was finishing up his prayers in the library.

Shlomi looked up from his prayer book. "When are you going to get another receptionist?" he said. "I'm not being paid enough for this job."

"Why don't you pray in the synagogue, like everybody else?"

Nick threw his suitcoat on the sofa, stood in the doorway of his office, facing Shlomi across the hall.

"I was hoping you'd come in early today," Shlomi said. "You could put on some *tefellin* and join me."

"Haven't worn them since I was thirteen—forgot how to put them on, how to read Hebrew."

"Come over here. I brought an extra pair for you. They were my father's."

Nick approached slowly. He eyed the ancient felt bag that contained the two leather praying devices that were used since the time of Moses. His own father's were similar. What had happened to them? He'd ask Marilee when he got home.

Shlomi removed the *tefellin* from the bag. "The first one, *yad*, hand, goes on your left arm, wound around the forearm seven times. Then around the hand and middle finger three times, then looped through and across, so." Shlomi fixed it to Nick's arm and hand while he spoke. "See how its winding spells one of God's names."

"What's it supposed to do?"

"Think of it as an antenna to heaven, for your connection to God. The other one, *rosh*, head, goes up here, so the box sits on your forehead, right at the hairline. You also need a yarmulke. Shlomi pulled a prayer skull cap from his pocket and put it on Nick's head, then placed the second *tefellin*.

"Am I plugged in now?" Nick said.

"Just about. We have to fine-tune your receiver." Shlomi slid the Hebrew prayer book on the table over to Nick. "Repeat after me, try to follow the Hebrew. *Barouch atau adonai...*"

The ancient prayer, the melody, the Hebrew letters, all slowly brought Nick to the edge of a meditative state. The sight of the leather straps wound around his arm opened his mind. He was in Jerusalem, at the Western Wall, the last remnant of the First and Second Temples of God. He knew the prayer's melody, he could read the Hebrew. Somehow, he knew.

"That was excellent for your first time in over thirty years," Shlomi said.

Nick's hands left the ancient stones of the wall.

His eyes opened. Without benefit of a jetliner, he was back in his office.

"Shlomi?"

"The prayers, you finished them on your own. We said them together."

"How long has it been?"

"A few minutes."

"Help me get these things off."

Shlomi unwound the leather straps, rewound them around the wooden prayer boxes they were connected to, and placed the *tefellin* back in the bag.

"Does that happen to you," Nick said, "when you pray with those on?"

"A real rush, huh?"

"If you call going over Niagara Falls in a paddleboat a rush. Do you do that every morning?"

"With the *minyan*—at *shul*. You're welcome to join us in the synagogue anytime."

"I don't know that I could handle it."

There was a pain on Nick's left biceps. He rubbed it, looked down.

Shlomi followed Nick's eyes.

"There's a bruise," Shlomi said. "I must have wound it too tightly on your arm."

"It wasn't on tight at all. Maybe God was trying to send me a message. I'll let you know about the synagogue," Nick said. "Got some calls to make. There's an ad in the *Preview* for a legal secretary. The phone should start ringing like crazy."

"Let's hope you get someone as good as Carol."

"Carol."

Nick breathed deeply. He went across the hall to his office, closed the door and sat at his desk.

The telephone rang several times before Nick realized he was the only one there to answer it.

"Shapiro law offices."

"Could I speak with Mr. Shapiro, please?" The woman's voice was institutional, working her way down a morning checklist of calls.

"Hold the line, please, I'll see if he's in." Nick changed the tone of his voice an octave lower. "Mr. Shapiro speaking."

"This is Angie, in accounting, at City National Bank? It's probably some kind of bookkeeping mistake in your office, Mr. Shapiro, but your check number 1402 to the phone company was returned for insufficient funds—"

"You must've made a mistake. There's more than three and a half million dollars in that account."

"The account's overdrawn, Mr. Shapiro. A withdrawal in that amount was made on Friday. Perhaps—"

"Someone...."

"Sir?"

Nick tried to speak, but the constriction in his throat would not allow it. Nick Shapiro, the lawyer who prided himself on attention to detail, had forgotten to remove Carol Emry as a signatory on the account.

"Mr. Shapiro?"

His breathing stopped, his face sweated he forced himself to take in air. He took in a gasp, chest pounding. Shapiro was too tough to cry over money—but this was more than just money. His words cracked, voice burning as if acid had been poured down his mouth.

"Tell the president, Robinson, I'll be there in ten minutes, an emergency."

"He's in meetings with the board of directors all morning—"

"My money's been stolen!"

Even as he said the words, Nick knew they might not be true. If Carol still had signature power, how could she be a thief?

He grabbed his coat and raced past the conference room toward the front door.

"Hey, where are the topless dancers?" Shlomi said.

"In hell."

Nick was already out the door.

CHAPTER 31

Nick pulled the car to a stop in front of his house. He couldn't remember the last twenty minutes of the drive home from the bank. How had he ended up at home?

He exited the car and slung his suitcoat over his shoulder. The videotape of his wife and Greeson stuck out from the side pocket, like an infected hangnail.

From the driveway, he could see through the front window. Marilee was shooing the children off to their bedrooms. She ran for the front door when she saw him, but it was too late—Nick had already turned the knob.

Marilee looked half-nervous, half-indignant. "What are you doing here?" she said.

Nick stepped into the living room foyer. He closed the door behind him.

"It's got something to do with the fact that I live here, remember?"

"You used to, remember? Now you're not allowed."

Marilee didn't know the divorce papers had not yet been served on Nick.

Nick lumbered his way over to the sofa and sank down in it, wanting to let himself disappear from sight in its cushions. He took the videotape from his coat pocket.

"This is a tape of you and Greeson."

Marilee scratched her forearms. She started for the tape, then stopped, keeping her distance from Nick.

"Dockett, that bastard."

"Guess you were getting even with me for all my prior infidelities," Nick said. "I could forgive you—the way you forgave me. If you stop seeing Greeson, maybe we could learn to love each other again. I'm going to need someone to love me after what's just happened."

Marilee's voice was shrill, almost insane. "I've already filed for the divorce. Don't you know? You've got three million dollars, and half of it is going to be mine."

"It's all gone," Nick said it almost as an afterthought.

Marilee went on as if she hadn't heard him. "Whether I stay with Greeson or not doesn't matter. After he finishes the case for me, I won't care. And don't think you can ruin me with that tape. Richard says it's inadmissible in evidence. You can watch it and jerk off to it if you like—you and that blackmailer Dockett."

Nick looked up. "Carol and Rene stole the money; there's nothing for either of us, just each other."

"Mr. Lawyer. Mr. Problem Solver—for everyone in the world but yourself. Do you expect me to believe anything so lame? My God."

"If only I were lying."

"The only truth is that Richard has a restraining order out on you. If you come within fifty yards of this house, I can have you arrested. The phone's right over there, I'll call the police."

"I want to see the children."

"They're at my mother's."

"I saw them through the window."

"They don't want to see you."

Nick stood. He headed for the children's bedrooms.

"I'm calling the police," Marilee said. She ran to the kitchen.

Nick opened Debbie's door. Both children were sitting on the edge of the bed. Tommy was sobbing. "Are you getting a divorce from Mom?" he managed to say between sniffles.

Nick sat between them. "I still love your mother—and I always will."

"I don't think she loves you, Dad," Debbie said. "I'm afraid."

"Nothing bad will ever happen to you," Nick said. "Neither of you."

He put his arms around the children, hugging them and bringing their heads in next to his with his hands.

"I'll have to move out for a while," Nick said. "Some place close by, we'll still be together."

Tommy wrapped his arms around Nick's waist and squeezed.

"If you hurry," Marilee said from the bedroom doorway, "you can get out of here before the police come. I'm sure you wouldn't want the children to see you taken out in handcuffs."

"No!" Tommy screamed.

Nick kissed the children's cheeks once more.

"Where will you go?" Debbie said.

Nick stood.

"For now, a place that may give me some answers."

"Can I come?" Tommy said.

"I wish you could, both of you."

Nick handed Marilee the only copy of the videotape, then he left his house.

CHAPTER 32

Shlomi's synagogue wasn't far from Nick's office.
It consisted of two adjoining houses fused together
by a wide hallway, with an extra addition in the
back for more seating. The building was far from
elegant, but its stabilizing force had kept the
neighborhood around Nick's office from going under altogether. Once inside the structure, it looked
like one of the cavernous, regal synagogues that
the rich Jews had built for themselves out in the
Highlands.

But those Jews weren't Orthodox.

Nick took one of the black silk skull caps from
the basket next to the door and placed it on his
head. It showed the respect of a Jewish man to
God by not baring his head to the heavens.

Straight ahead, past a narrow wooden hallway,
was the empty sanctuary. It held a hundred seats,
which didn't seem possible from the outside. Nick
moved forward to it. A voice came from a room off
to the side.

Nick went to the doorway of the room, then
stepped inside.

A short man with a bushy, gray beard was
standing at the end of a long table that was surrounded by other men in beards, sitting. It was a

library of some sort, and the man was giving a lecture. He stopped in midsentence.

Everyone stared up at Nick in silence.

"It's O.K.," Shlomi said from his seat at the table. "I know him."

The speaker went back to his lecture.

Shlomi stood, came to Nick. "Come," he said, "we can talk in the sanctuary."

On the way they passed a glass-enclosed showcase containing a collection of ancient menorahs. One of the synagogue's members owned the display and showed it all over the country. This month it was at its home base. Nick stopped to stare, but Shlomi took him by the arm, easing him along.

"You look like shit," Shlomi said. He looked up at the front of the sanctuary, where the Torah scrolls were contained in the ark, and muttered an apology in Hebrew. "Sit," he said to Nick.

They both sat in folding chairs in the middle of the room.

"I need help," Nick said.

"I wish I needed your kind of help." Shlomi uttered more words in Hebrew. "You've got more money than G-d."

Nick took Shlomi by the arm. "The money's gone. Carol and Rene stole it from me. My wife's having an affair with her divorce attorney. She's not going to let me see my children. My life is over. What I want to know from you is if there's any way to commit suicide, so my soul will still go to heaven?"

"You need to talk to the rabbi, Nick."

"I want to talk you."

"Jewish law doesn't sanction suicide—so get it out of your mind."

"What about the mass suicide at Masada, so the Romans couldn't kill the Jews? Wasn't that sanctioned?"

"No...I don't know. Stop talking nonsense. We're in a house that celebrates the glory of life. If you've come to me for advice about that, I can help."

"Meditate some more? I don't think so."

"Something else."

"Grow a beard and side curls and dress funny?"

"Not necessarily."

"I didn't come here for riddles, either."

"Go to Israel for a while. Pray at the Western Wall, the closest place to God a Jew is allowed to get these days. The answers will come to you then."

Nick shook his head. "Just like magic."

"I'll look after things at the office, don't worry. Do what I say, go."

"I've got to be here. The police, the money, my divorce case, the kids—"

"Go. If I'm wrong—"

"Then I'll kill myself."

"Then, you'll have my permission."

How many times had he made this trip down-town? A thousand? Five thousand? Nick tried to remember during the drive. It was as if his life was unfolding before his eyes as he drove. Where had twenty-five years gone?

He parked in the cheap lot by the river flats, not even remembering how he had gotten there.

"Five bucks," the sun-wrinkled attendant said, "in advance." The man's cellular telephone looked as if it had grown into the side of his head. He was talking about football scores to someone on the other end.

"I'll pay when I get back," Nick said. "If I come back."

"A wise guy," the attendant said into the phone, "hold on a minute, Joe." He puffed on a cigarette and looked at Nick. "Look, mister. The money now, or beat it."

"Be careful how you talk to a man who doesn't care about life anymore, sonny."

Nick brushed him aside and continued on.

The attendant shrugged his shoulders and went back to his conversation.

Nick felt strange being downtown without a coat and tie—or a briefcase. He had tried to order the airline tickets over the phone, but the travel agent he'd used for years, whose office was near the courthouse, insisted he come down with a credit card.

Wonderful thing, credit cards. It's what people use when they don't have any money. And now Nick had very little of that.

Nick looked down at himself to see if his pants were still on—he felt naked walking beneath the tall buildings. They were staring down at him. What was a lawyer doing walking in their midst if he wasn't going to perform his craft at the courthouse? The skyscrapers knew they could see.

From force of habit Nick turned left on Galtier Street, then checked himself and went right. The agency was still two blocks down.

"Hi, Mr. Shapiro, remember me?"

The feminine voice came from the edge of the sidewalk nearest the office buildings. Nick stopped, turned to see the bikini hot dog lady. She was no longer wearing her swimsuit—it had been replaced by knee-length shorts.

"You're overdressed," Nick said.

She rolled a string of hot dogs on the grill with a spatula. "I tried to call you last week, Mr. Shapiro. All the franchise owners got problems. City's forcing regulations down our throats—where we can sell, what we can't wear—"

"You'd better call a lawyer."

"I thought you were." She handed Nick a hot

dog in a bun. "Here, on the house."

"Is it kosher?"

"Sure—it's from a circumcised pig."

Nick took a bite. "Liked you better in the bi-kini."

"You and everyone else. Revenue's dropped off big-time since the change. How much would you charge to represent us all, Mr. Shapiro?"

"Three million dollars."

"What was in that hot dog?"

"Poison, I hope."

She moved a little closer to Nick, and swayed her body around, the way women with great figures do.

"Maybe you could come to my place tonight to discuss the case. I could make you a real dinner."

Nick closed his eyes for a minute, wondered what it might be like.

"Love to, but I have to go kill myself now. Maybe afterwards."

"Sure."

"Thanks for the hot dog," Nick said.

Another customer moved between them to examine the grill.

The hot dog lady turned her head around the man and saw Nick as he walked away.

"You've got my card if you change your mind, Mr. Shapiro."

"I have no mind left to change," Nick said over his shoulder.

Three hours later a big jet roared its way down the tarmac of the Harris County Airport. It was the part of flying that Nick had always hated the most. Would the thing get airborne? There was a final bumping sound that was either the tail of the fuselage pounding off the ground, or the wheels retracting. Nick could never tell the difference. His palms always dripped with sweat thinking it was the former.

It was a smooth takeoff, and soon the plane was soaring out across the river, the wind at its back. The East was behind them. Then the pilot made a wide turn, banking off on the wind, in the direction of the Holy Land.

The cloudless late afternoon provided a perfect view of the ground. Nick looked down. The landmarks were familiar—the series of parks leading away from the riverbanks, the water tower, a block away from that, his house.

At age fifty, Neal Shapiro was on his way to Israel, alone—no family, no friends, no money—to find the meaning of life.

He drifted off into a deep sleep, where, sometimes, even the craziest things made sense.

CHAPTER 33

After a flight of more than seven hours, the jumbo jet had crossed the Atlantic, waved down to the British Isles, then Portugal, and was cruising over the Spanish countryside for its final destination, Madrid.

Jerry Dockett was awakened by the first rays of morning sunlight coming through the plane's porthole. He stretched, yawned, rolled his tongue around the inside of his mouth, and remembered that he had not spent the night at home.

He had missed Rene's direct flight by minutes at the Harris County Airport, and nearly had a fistfight with the ticket taker who wouldn't let him make a dash down the connecting ramp for a dive at her departing plane. He'd gotten the next flight to New York, made the transfer there. His passport was in his briefcase—along with other essentials of his trade, including a disassembled, case-hardened plastic revolver and plastic bullets that couldn't be detected by airport X-rays. The gun was courtesy of a mob hood he once arrested; Jerry didn't bother to turn it in to the evidence clerk at the station.

"Would you like a hot towel for your face?" the dark-skinned flight attendant said in a Spanish accent. She held the steaming towel out in front of Dockett with a pair of tongs.

"What time is it?" Dockett said.

"Six forty-five."

Dockett took the towel and wiped his face.

"Morning or night?"

She pointed out the window. "When the sun comes up, it is morning."

Dockett stretched his neck toward the cabin ceiling, smiled at the stewardess and waited for her to smile back.

"If an American woman got off a plane in Madrid without a hotel reservation," Dockett said, "where do you think she'd stay?"

"I would stay at El Cid—nice, but not too expensive, overlooking a park in the center of town. A beautiful statue of Cervantes is there."

"Any banks in the area?"

"The hotel is surrounded by them."

Dockett scratched the back of his head. "I need some coffee."

"Hotel El Cid," Dockett said to the cab driver.

"*Qual El Cid, señor?*" Which El Cid?

"Cervantes."

"Ah, *si*, Don Quixote."

It was the only town Dockett had ever been in where all the cabs were clean, air conditioned and were Mercedes.

The drive from the airport was a sea of contrasts: ancient, medieval buildings mixed in with modern skyscrapers; bands of Gypsies camped in tents next to expensive looking apartment complexes. There were even international banks side by side with mom and pop currency exchange booths.

Dockett was certain the cabbie had driven him

in circles for the last ten minutes.

Finally, the taxi stopped in front of the El Cid Hotel, across from a dusty park, where the only patches of grass were occupied by street dogs.

Dockett stuck a twenty dollar bill in the driver's face.

"Take American?"

"*Pesetas, señor.*"

"Take this and wait. I'll change money inside."

Dockett was back in minutes, but the taxi was gone. The ten dollar cab ride had just cost twice as much. So much for the integrity of Spanish cabbies.

Dockett went back to the hotel lobby.

A young man in a blue blazer came to him.

"*Buenos dias, señor.*"

"Is there an American woman, Rene Handeman, staying here?"

"We can only give that sort of information to the police, or to other guests of the hotel."

"I'll take a single room for a week."

"Certainly."

The clerk signed Dockett up, checked his passport, and took an impression of his credit card."

"What about the woman?" Dockett said.

The clerk slid his thumb through a Rolodex.

"She is not here, señor. I am sorry."

"So am I."

Dockett picked up the room key, one of those electronic punch cards, then took the lift up to the fifth floor.

The room was the size of a small closet. If Henny Youngman were there, Dockett knew what he'd say: even the mice were hunchback. At least it had its own bathroom and shower.

Dockett turned on the hot water and got in. He did his best thinking there.

He shampooed his scalp hard, as if to get the cobwebs out of his brain. If he were back in the States, finding Rene would be routine: a skip-trace, a few drive-bys, a fin or a sawbuck here and there and he'd be knocking on her door.

But Madrid?

He got out of the shower and toweled himself off while standing in front of the window that overlooked the park. The iron-work statue of Cervantes was rusting where the black paint had worn off, but the tourists were already flocking to take pictures of each other beneath it.

Then the bell in Dockett's head rang.

The telephone call back to Harris County took several minutes and the line was fuzzy, but Carol's voice was recognizable.

"Where are you?" Carol said.

"Where they eat tappas and dance the flamenco like fish swim. Have you got Rene's passport number, a picture of her, that sort of thing?"

"Yeah."

"Look, call the travel agent, find out if Rene booked through them. If she did, lie to them, do whatever you have to find out if she went to Spain."

Carol hesitated before she spoke. "It's two in the morning here."

"Then wake up the agent at home. Be creative. Call me back, I'll be waiting."

Dockett gave her the hotel's number from the back of a match book on the table.

The ring sounded funny, not like any Dockett had heard before. It took several bleats to wake him from the slumber in which he'd fallen.

"She's in Madrid," Carol said.

"At least we've got the right haystack." Dockett's voice was still thick.

"Even if you find her," Carol said, "it's probably already too late; she's hidden the money by now."

"In this business, it's never too late. Fax me the information, her birth certificate, passport number, a photo."

"How can I find a fax machine at this hour?"

"You still have the keys to Nick's office, don't you? And Carol, don't tell Nick about any of this—I'll explain it to you later."

For one thing, the authorities would want to know why the picture of Dockett's "wife" was xeroxed in black and white. He'd have to do a lot of thinking on his feet. For him, going to the police for help was like asking a Colombian money launderer to do your shirts. But he had no choice. If Rene was still in Madrid, he had to find her fast, before it was too late.

Dockett had waited on a hard wooden bench in front of the booking desk for twenty minutes before they found a detective who could speak English. Other than the language difference, the place seemed to function a lot like a police station in Middle America, only without the jelly doughnuts.

A short, balding man in his forties came out from a side door. He stood and looked around the waiting room.

"Mr. Handeman?" he said, in choppy English.

Dockett stood and came to him.

"I can't tell you how worried I am about my wife," Dockett said. "I hope you can help."

The Spanish cop shook Dockett's hand.

"My name is Nemsis. We usually have to find the husband. They seem to become lost a lot more—in certain sections of Madrid. Come to my office where we can speak more freely."

Dockett followed him through a labyrinth of hallways and makeshift, partitioned offices with shaky metal desks that contained manual typewriters and the occasional outdated computer.

"The more seasoned officers, like me, have the nice offices in the back—where the air-conditioning sometimes works."

The office was small, the size of Dockett's hotel room, with a picture of a pretty teenage girl adorning the wall and nothing more. Dockett didn't inquire.

"And what do think happened to your wife?" Nemsis asked from behind his desk.

"I was supposed to meet her at Bank Leumi; it's an international Israeli banking chain—"

"I'm familiar with it."

"We were going to transfer some funds through the Madrid branch to Israel—for an investment we're making there."

"An investment?"

"It's nothing much, a condominium in Jerusalem."

"I see."

"I got to the bank, and she wasn't there. I waited, but she never came."

"What did your hotel say when you inquired there?"

"We'd already checked out of the hotel."

"And you're prepared to show me your airline tickets to confirm your departure from the country?"

"We're not leaving Spain."

"Staying in Madrid with no hotel?"

Dockett curled his toes inside his size twelve shoes. "We were to join a bus tour for a week's travel around the country. The members of the tour met with the director at the hotel for a cocktail party last night."

"Did you or your wife know anybody else on the tour, Mr. Handeman?"

Dockett didn't answer.

"Mr. Handeman?"

"Well, there was someone—an old friend who I thought was out of the picture."

"I see."

"He just showed up from the States—looked to me like it was planned."

Nemsis took a long look at the picture on the wall.

"People sometimes act strangely on holiday, especially when they're so far from home. Spanish wine may be too strong for them. Give me your wife's picture, her passport information. I think we can get to the bottom of this—affair."

"I hope you find her quickly; she means everything to me."

"Can't live with them, or without them, eh, Mr. Handeman?"

"Something like that."

Dockett woke the next morning, had a continental breakfast at the El Cid Hotel, then waited in the lobby with an American newspaper. At 11:00 a.m. the clerk behind the reception desk answered the telephone, placed a hand over the receiver and looked out over the lobby.

"*Señor* Handeman?"

At first Dockett didn't remember his cover. Then he looked up from the paper. "That's me."

"Telephone, *señor*. You may take it over there." The clerk pointed to a nearby table.

Dockett picked up the phone, made sure the clerk hung his up before he spoke.

"Handeman," Dockett said.

"Nemsis here. We have some...news for you. But perhaps you would like to come to the station so we can speak personally—these things can sometimes be difficult."

"She's not—hurt, is she?" Dockett said.

"It is nothing like that."

"Then tell me. I must know now."

"I have to remind you, Mr. Handeman, that the penalties in Spain for assault against another man are much stronger than in your country. Use any type of weapon, and the courts here will throw away the key to your prison cell."

"Tell me."

"Your wife has checked into the Hotel Agumar."

Dockett hesitated a moment for effect.

"Is she...with someone?"

"We don't know that for certain—the room is registered in her name. But please, for everyone's sake, keep your head, whatever you may find."

"Don't worry, detective. When I see her, I'll keep it."

"I wish you luck, my friend. I have been in your position myself."

"I don't think so, Detective Nemsis."

CHAPTER 34

The Hotel Agumar was on a busy wide avenue one block from the Royal Palace. Behind the hotel and the buildings that adjoined it was a steep cliff, below which were vast forests still owned by the king. In ancient times they were the king's hunting grounds, now it was his golf course. Guests of the Agumar had playing privileges, if they wanted to pay the $300 greens fee.

Dockett entered the lobby of the Agumar looking too big and sweaty to belong. He was the extra-ugly American. He headed for the bar in the center of the lobby and ordered a beer. There had been no time to make a plan. Perhaps by the end of the beer—only one—something might come to him.

Dockett surveyed the room. Rene wasn't wasting any time spending Nick's money. The hotel smelled of wealth. Tall, slim ladies dressed in expensive designer clothing, possessing face and boob jobs, walked about with their entourage of servants, poodle dogs and men with thin mustaches close behind. Young curvy women in sun robes that covered their bikini bathing suits got off the elevators and were walking out toward the swimming pool.

The king had a good view of the pool from the palace balcony.

Instead of trying to find out her room number by conning the desk clerk, Dockett would wait for Rene to come to him. It wasn't good luck to press your luck.

A half hour and three beers later, Rene stepped from the elevator wearing a tight sun dress over her swimsuit. The oversized sunglasses did nothing to disguise her. There weren't many woman who had a body that looked like hers.

Normally, after three beers, Dockett was either too horny or too groggy to concentrate on work. For a big guy, he couldn't hold his liquor.

He stood up from the bar without feeling any effects. "Stuff's bullpiss," he said to the Spanish bartender.

The bartender smiled, scooped Dockett's tip from the counter. "*Singa tu madre.*" Fuck your mother.

If Dockett knew what the bartender had said, he would have skewered him through the testicles with one of the toreador picks that hung above the bar. Instead, Dockett smiled back.

He walked across the lobby to a small gift shop and purchased one of those floppy cotton doughboy hats. He pulled the front down low over his face. He went out to the pool.

In a corner by herself, away from the competition, Rene was stretched out long on a chaise lounge on the other side of the pool.

Off to the side, Dockett sat at a table with an umbrella. There was a great view of the king's woods, the palace—and Rene.

When the waiter came around, Dockett ordered another beer.

Rene made a show of applying the sunscreen

to her skin. She set the lotion bottle down on the table next to her—with its top off.

"Mind if I do your back?" Dockett said, standing over her.

"What the...Dockett?"

"Always thought you'd look great in a two-piece, probably much better in a no piece." Dockett pulled up a chair, sat and started applying the lotion to Rene's back. "I don't advise a scene, Rene."

"Why are you here?"

"So you don't get a sunburn."

"Nick sent you."

"Think what you like—us two have got some talking to do."

"I could scream, call a cop."

"I could kill you, too."

"Poison me with suntan lotion?"

"I've got a gun in my pocket." Dockett showed her the bulge of the plastic pistol.

"And I thought you were just happy to see me."

"Cut the shit, Rene. Get up slowly, slip that little dress over your pretty head, and lead me up to your room."

Rene's penthouse suite had a magnificent view of the forest, and beyond, to the rolling Spanish countryside that met the city without any suburbs in between.

Dockett locked the door and made Rene give him the key.

"There're plenty of women in Harris County," Rene said. "You didn't have to come all the way to Spain to put the moves on me."

"We could do that too, if you want."

"I might want."

Rene sat on the cushy leather sofa, not minding that her skirt was looking more and more like a belt.

"But you know that's not why I came," Dockett said, after taking a long look at her legs.

"I only know you're holding me against my will, and that's a crime in any country," Rene said.

"That's right, I almost forgot. You're a lawyer. Then tell me this counsellor: what's the penalty for first-degree fraud, grand theft and embezzlement?"

"Why, whatever do you mean?"

Dockett slapped her hard across the face with the back of his hand.

"We can do this the hard way, or the very hard way. It's up to you."

Rene spit a combination of saliva and blood at Dockett. "That hurt, asshole."

"Poor baby. I used to be a cop, remember? In the old days we knew how to make people talk fast, especially women. Cigarette butts on pretty pink nipples. They don't stay pink for long. Do you like yours medium or rare?"

"I don't eat meat."

"That's not what I heard."

"Bastard."

"You know why I'm here, Rene. Nick's money. I want it back."

"What are you going to do if I just zip up, tell you nothing?"

Dockett took a cigarette from the pack and lit it.

"You're a beautiful woman, Rene. But I don't care about that anymore. There are more important things in life. Only a fool kills for a woman. I kill for money. The money, Rene."

Dockett moved closer to her. She could feel the fire in the cigarette.

"The money—if I did have it—would be well hidden away by now. An account in some country where bankers know how to keep secrets."

"Maybe—if you didn't think someone would be right on your scent. And that's what you thought, Rene. No, the money's still right here in Spain, all those pretty pesetas, just waiting for you to send them wherever in the world you might want—or maybe share it with some brave, well-hung matador right here in Madrid."

"I'll just shut up."

Dockett pulled the white plastic gun from his pocket, silencer and all. He wasted no time firing a muffled shot at Rene's left thigh.

The gunflash and "poof" sound startled her almost as much as the pain of the through-and-through flesh wound, just above the femur bone. The bleeding was slow at first, then started to spurt with each heartbeat, like a cheap patio fountain.

"You want to live more than I want the money, right, Rene?"

"Help me. I'm bleeding to death."

Dockett ripped off her dress in one pull. He tied it tight around her leg, just above the wound.

"You won't die," Dockett said, "not yet."

Rene's face cringed. "Christ." She tried not to look at the blood.

Dockett fired another shot across Rene's scalp. The bullet formed a perfect part through the side of her hair, almost as if it had been combed in. There was only a small trail of blood.

"Your hairdresser couldn't do that good," Dockett said. Rene screamed.

Dockett stuffed a small pillow from the sofa in her mouth. He opened his briefcase and took out an official-looking paper.

"This is the Spanish equivalent of a power of attorney," Dockett said. "A nice Madrid policeman, who felt sorry for me, gave me the name of a crooked lawyer—you know all about them—the lawyer prepared a prenotarized power of attorney. All you have to do is sign it and tell me the name of the bank where the money is. Then you can live." He pulled the pillow from her mouth.

Rene's face had turned ashen. After several deep breaths, she seemed to regain her senses, understand how close to the edge she was.

"Banco Nacional," she said, in a semiwhisper.

"You're halfway home," Dockett said. He held out a pen. "Now sign."

Rene wrote her name on the line.

Dockett put the paper back in the briefcase.

"I should finish the job on you," Dockett said. "But I'm a gentleman."

He touched her between the legs with the barrel of the gun, and ran it back and forth for a moment.

Then he ripped the telephone line from the wall and tied Rene's hands and feet with it. He shoved the pillow back in her mouth.

"That should hold you until tomorrow, when the maid comes in, if you don't bleed to death first. You shouldn't, the tourniquet's good. Hope you speak Spanish, she can be the first to hear how you went from riches to rags. Have a nice life, Rene."

Rene's head slumped between her knees. She was looking at the thing that usually got her out of trouble. Now she could only dream.

The last thing she heard was the turning of the key in the door lock.

CHAPTER 35

The old woman's voice had a heavy European accent; she sounded like Nick's grandmother. Her face was the image of his mother, warm, smiling, despite its age. Nick had never believed in reincarnation, but after six months of living in Anna Goldberg's house in Jerusalem, he was changing his mind.

"Neal," she called from across the tomato and cucumber garden, "bring the fertilizer, I can't lift the bag."

Nick was bent at the waist, so his hands could dig into the earth. He stood, slapped flesh together, until the dirt came off. He wiped his brow where the bright sun hit it, looked down the slope of the hill from Anna's house, to the walls of the Old City. Each time he saw it, he thought of the ancient temples, where it was said the God of his people had dwelt.

"I can't find it," Nick said.

"Behind the melons," Anna said. "Hurry, I got *gadampta* flesh, pot roast, in the oven; it shouldn't overcook."

Nick dropped his trowel in the ground. He brushed some grape vines out of the way and headed toward the melons.

When he'd first gotten off the plane at Ben Gurion Airport in Tel Aviv, he had no idea what he was going to do, where he would stay. He took a bus to Deizengoff Street and sat, suitcase in hand, at a sidewalk cafe drinking a Coke and watching the bustle of a city that was alive with the joy of life, despite the terrorism it experienced.

After three Cokes, a falafel sandwich, and a case of heartburn that he thought would kill him, Nick was sorry he'd come to Israel. The saying was true: you can't run away from your problems.

That's when he met Anna.

She was on the sidewalk, holding four heavy shopping bags in her hands, filled with everything from groceries to her laundry. She asked Nick to help her lug them onto a public bus that had stopped just outside the cafe, heading to her house in Jerusalem—she had asked first in Hebrew, then English. It was the beginning of a wonderful symbiotic relationship: Nick helped Anna, a widow, with chores around the house; in exchange, he got a free room—and the best cooking he'd had since his grandmother died when he was a boy.

"Here's your fertilizer, Anna. I don't know why you bother. This soil's so rich, you don't need it."

"It's what gives the radishes such a sweet taste."

Nick could never eat radishes back in the States. Here, they were succulent.

"Now you tell me, Anna, how does cow manure do that?"

"Because it's from God's chosen cows."

Nick laughed.

"It's good to see you smile once in a while, Neal. I was beginning to worry." Anna dished out a handful of fertilizer onto the ground. "Why don't you try calling your children? Don't you miss them?"

They were what he missed the most.

"When the time is right," Nick said.

"And your wife?"

He didn't tell Anna about the final judgment of divorce he had received in the post.

"All right," Anna said. "I'll go in and check on dinner. You should take a walk to the Western Wall tonight, place a note in the cracks. It might help. God reads all of the notes. I know."

Nick sat back on a wooden bench behind the garden on the hill. He let his arms rest on the backing, looking out over the Old City. How could he feel so at home there, even though his family was so far away? If only the children could be there with him, to grow up in a country where they had nothing to fear, despite the dangers all around.

Anna came out to the garden from the side door, bent at the waist a bit, feet shuffling. She was holding several envelopes.

"A letter from home for you," she said.

When Nick was in the army, a letter from home was better than money.

Anna handed him the envelope, turned and made her way slowly back to the house.

The letter wasn't from the children. There was no return address.

Nick sliced it open with the sharp edge of the trowel.

It was from Jerry Dockett, a cashiers' check, no note, for $3,300,000. Dockett had taken out a hundred thousand.

Anna stuck her head out the door. "Neal...Neal, I've been calling you. Dinner's ready. What are you going to do?"

Nick breathed in the Israeli air deeply and smiled.

"Try to get my life back, Anna. The way it was a long time ago. I guess that was my plan from the beginning. I just didn't know it."

Anna stepped outside of her house and saw Nick holding the check. "Happiness can't be bought, like groceries at the corner market, Neal."

Nick hesitated for a moment, then looked out at the walls of the Old City below. "It can, if you shop at the right store."

"Are you going home, Neal?"

"Yes, Anna, I'm going home."

"What if it's true, that a person can never go home again, Neal?"

Nick ran his fingers over the raised type of the dollar sign on his check. "In America, Anna, anything is possible, even going home again."

About The Author

Born in St. Paul, Minnesota, Michael Lechtman earned a bachelor's degree in psychology from the University of Minnesota. After serving in the army as a second lieutenant, he graduated from the University of Miami School of Law. He has practiced both criminal and civil law. He is currently practicing family law and writing his next novel. Married with two children, he resides in Florida.

WATCH FOR THESE NEW COMMONWEALTH BOOKS

WATCH FOR THESE NEW COMMONWEALTH BOOKS

WATCH FOR THESE NEW COMMONWEALTH BOOKS

	ISBN #	U.S.	Can
❑ **RIBBONS AND ROSES**, D.B. Taylor	1-55197-088-0	$4.99	$6.99
❑ **PRISON DREAMS**, John O. Powers	1-55197-039-2	$4.99	$6.99
❑ **A VOW OF CHASTITY**, Marcia Jean Greenshields	1-55197-106-2	$4.99	$6.99
❑ **LAVENDER'S BLUE**, Janet Tyers	1-55197-058-9	$4.99	$6.99
❑ **HINTS AND ALLEGATIONS**, Kimberly A. Dascenzo	1-55197-073-2	$4.99	$6.99
❑ **BROKEN BRIDGES**, Elizabeth Gorlay	1-55197-119-4	$4.99	$6.99
❑ **PAINTING THE WHITE HOUSE**, Hal Marcovitz	1-55197-095-3	$4.99	$6.99
❑ **THE KISS OF JUDAS**, J.R. Thompson	1-55197-045-7	$4.99	$6.99
❑ **BALLARD'S WAR**, Tom Holzel	1-55197-112-7	$4.99	$6.99
❑ **ROSES FOR SARAH**, Anne Philips	1-55197-125-9	$4.99	$6.99
❑ **THE TASKMASTER**, Mary F. Murchison	1-55197-113-5	$4.99	$6.99
❑ **SECOND TIME**, Thomas E. Sprain	1-55197-135-6	$4.99	$6.99
❑ **MY BROTHER'S TOWN**, B.A. Stuart	1-55197-138-0	$4.99	$6.99
❑ **MISSING PIECES**, Carole W. Holden	1-55197-172-0	$4.99	$6.99
❑ **DIARY OF A GHOST**, Alice Richards Laule	1-55197-132-1	$4.99	$6.99

Available at your local bookstore or use this page to order.

Send to: COMMONWEALTH PUBLICATIONS INC.
9764 - 45th Avenue
Edmonton, Alberta, CANADA T6E 5C5

Please send me the items I have checked above. I am enclosing
$_____ (please add $2.50 per book to cover postage and handling). Send check or money order, no cash or C.O.D.'s, please.

Mr./Mrs./Ms._____

Address_____

City/State_____ Zip_____

Please allow four to six weeks for delivery.
Prices and availability subject to change without notice.

The case of a lifetime has come to lawyer Neal Shapiro: a baby killed in a car crash, and there's plenty of insurance money. Fighting two-bit divorces and corrupt judges all of his career, Shapiro plans to retire on this case. But his plan unravels when trusted associates lie and steal, and his wife cheats on him. They drag Shapiro down as low as he can go—until he learns that the meaning of life is not money, but to fight his way back up.

Shapiro's Plan

by
Michael Lechtman